When the Mapou Sings

Nadine Pinede

CANDLEWICK PRESS

Pour Manman
Wòch mwen an

Copyright © 2024 by Nadine Pinede
Epigraph copyright 1938 from
Tell My Horse by Zora Neale Hurston

First edition 2024

Library of Congress Catalog Card Number 2024935389
ISBN 978-1-5362-3566-1

24 25 26 27 28 29 APS 10 9 8 7 6 5 4 3 2 1

Printed in Humen, Dongguan, China

This book was typeset in Brioso Pro and Akaya Kanadaka.

Candlewick Press
99 Dover Street
Somerville, Massachusetts 02144

www.candlewick.com

This incident struck me as strange, the more I thought
about it. It was not usual for Lucille not to want
to do anything I wanted done because she loved to
please. Already I was beginning to love her and to
depend upon her. Later on I put her on the roster of
my few earthly friends and gave her all my faith.

—Zora Neale Hurston, *Tell My Horse*

Wòch nan dlo
pa konn doulè wòch nan soley.

Stones in the water
don't know the pain of stones in the sun.

—Haitian proverb

Manman

My birth
brought your death

your blood
a lavalas
in rainy season.

Papa buried the placenta
with orange seeds
and watered them
with tears.

Papa told me
you were a Mother Tree
and your great-grandmother
was a princess,
from the first people
who named us
Ayiti,
the Land of Mountains.
She fell in love with a mawon,
a runaway who hid in caves
and climbed mountains
to freedom,
then returned with his princess
to fight the French.

Papa does his best
    to hide
the ashes
in his heart.

He makes tables, chairs,
cedar coffins
to sell in his shop.

Your older sister, Tante Lila,
never married.

She moved in with us.

When she braids my hair
it's always too tight.
The dresses she sews
hang loose on my body,
as thin as a gazelle.

Whatever she cooks
always needs salt.
Not like Cousin Phebus,
whose food
makes our tongues dance.

Tante Lila prays the rosary
every day,
scolds me
when I climb
my favorite mapou,
the sacred tree.

> So I keep
> our secret.
>
> How in the forest
> when I touch the trees—
> barks grainy, knotted,
> or peeled slick smooth—

I see shapes in the wood
calling me to carve them.
I feel the heartbeat of their roots
pulse through my bare feet.

The trees sing to me.

Inside each one
of them

a tiny spark

of

you.

PART ONE
LAKAY

Friendliness and Understanding

AUGUST 15, 1934
HINCHE, HAITI

> *Statement from the Secretary of State:*
> *In the nearly twenty years during which our marine and*
> *naval forces have been stationed in Haiti they have rendered*
> *invaluable, disinterested service to the Haitian Government*
> *and the people. At this present moment they are withdrawing*
> *from the island in an atmosphere of great friendliness and*
> *the best of understanding. We wish for the Government and*
> *people of Haiti stability, progress and all success.*

When the section chief
finishes reading to us,
gathered in the muggy heat,
no one says a word.

Was he expecting applause?

They say the section chief—
at first respected,
now detested—
helped sòlda Ameriken yo
kill Caco resisters
steal our land
and force us like slaves
to build roads.

"Friendliness and understanding? Hmph."
The air is thick
with resentment
and relief.

Surely things will be better now.

For the first time in my fourteen years,
I see the Haitian flag raised
from its lower position at half-mast,
and the drapo Ameriken an,
always higher till now,
lowered, folded,
and taken away.

My Friend Fifina

I'll never forget
the first time I saw her
when the school year started.

In the courtyard   of the Mission School
I sat   apart from the others

drawing a bird
in red earth with a twig
from Mapou.

"That's beautiful."

Her voice arrived first,
warm honey and butter.

I looked up and saw skin
the color of glowing dark walnut
her soft cheve swa
a silky braid down her back.

A marabou,
those we consider
the most beautiful.

"I'm Fifina."

I stood up, wiped my hands
on my skirt.

"I'm Lucille."

We walked back to the classroom

inside me

a sunrise.

Trust

At the Bassin Zim waterfall,
where Papa taught me to swim
in the rivière Samana

and dive in underwater caves,
the light-jeweled water
caresses the cliff.

I teach Fifina to swim,
first holding her
as she floats on her back
her black hair fanning out
like angel wings.

When I sense
her body relax,
trust the water,
I let go.

Listen

Fifina and I perch
high like birds
on Mapou's branches
for hours.

I press my ear
against the side stripes
of Mapou's bark,
Fifina next to me.

"Don't you hear anything?"

Her mouth
rises in a smile,
but she
never laughs at me

never makes me feel
my head's not on straight

never says
that I look like a boy.

"I don't hear anything,"
says Fifina.

"If I told you
Mapou sings to me,
what would you think?"

"I'd think you're lucky!
Tell me what you hear,"
she says.

"I hear a woman's voice singing,
and when I close my eyes,

behind my eyelids
I see flashing lights,
like bird wings
fluttering in the sun.

"It doesn't make sense
until I fall asleep.
Then they all come together
in my dreams. I used to
try and draw them,
but now I want to carve,
like Papa."

Fifina holds my hand
and squeezes it.

"You have a gift."

"Promise you won't tell anyone?"

"I promise."

That makes me smile,
our secret to keep.

Our feet swing free
from Mapou's branches.

We talk of what

shape our lives will be

when we start our own school

where girls will learn

more than we do at the Mission School.

We'll make our own book,
with her mother's leaf-medicine recipes
and my drawings of the plants.

We'll teach girls how to carve, sew, draw, climb trees.
We'll teach girls the songs of trees, flowers, birds, butterflies,
the sun, moon, mountains, clouds.

Mapou listens
to our dreams
falling like gentle rain
on her leaves.

When it's time to go home

we climb down   carefully

                Mapou's branch in my hand
                to chase away
                snakes.

Mine

Each mapou
is special,
a resting place
reposwa

for the ones before us
still with us,
ever since our land
born from fire
stood up high from the sea
to make mountains
behind mountains.

Those who serve the spirits
say they know exactly
what makes mapou trees sacred.

"Trees are God's creation,
but He made them mute,"
says Sister Gilberte
when I tell her
about my Mapou.

"The Church or the spirits,
you can't serve them both."

To stay in school,
I keep my silence.

Still,
Mapou sings to me.

Days of Blood

"Bonjou, Ti Sè!"
Fifina calls out.
She calls me Little Sister,
which I love.

We're both the same age,
but
she looks more
like
a grown woman.

"Bonjou, Fifina."

Her name
a swelling sail
in the wind.

Today she stands
as I climb my beloved
Mapou.

"Come on."
I stretch out my hand.

She shakes her head
looks down at her feet.

"I can't anymore,
because of the cloth."

"What cloth?"

"To catch the blood
between my legs.
It's pinned to my panties
but if I move too much
the blood trickles down.
I have two
so I can boil the other
clean with soap."

My stomach starts churning,
bubbling with nausea.

So that's what's different.
I can smell her blood,
mingled with sweat and soap.

Will she start thinking of
boys and babies,

and forget our school
and me?

"How long
 do you bleed?"

"It only lasts a week,"
 she says.

"Seven whole days?
 Doesn't it hurt?"

"It did at first,
 but Manman held me
 when I cried.

"She said the bleeding was
 the song of the moon
 in my body.

"Then she made me a tizan
 from wild mushrooms and herbs.
 It helped with the pain.

"Don't be afraid,
 Ti Sè.

"I'll tell you
 my mother's recipe,
 when your days
 of blood begin."

I close my eyes
 to fight   tears
            fear
            anger.

Nothing will ever

make me stop climbing
or carving.

Carving

With a knife

    in my hand

        I don't think.

As I carve next to Papa,
    on a smaller stool,
        he stops from time to time
           to look at my work.
Sometimes
    he nods his encouragement
        or says "not bad"
           or a rare "well done."

I happily hum

    those little songs

        those lullabies

           inside me

                around me

        beneath and above.

        Songs of the Mother Tree.

        Pine or cedar,

        oak or mahogany

mostly I carve

birds.

Or the same two shapes.

One sun-round face.

One black full moon

in her arms.

A mother whose face
I can't remember
and whose songs
I can't forget.

Drawing Numbers in the Air

Thank goodness
Fifina helps me
with math.

If the Sisters knew
how bad I am at it,
they might give up on me,

although they say
math is for boys
and we don't need to learn
it as much.

Fifina disagrees,
like Cousin Phebus.

I especially hate
multiplication and long division.

The numbers can't stay in place
long enough for me to calculate.

To see them
and hold them in place,
I have to write them in the air
with my index finger.

Fifina never laughs at me
when she knows
I'm doing this
under the desk.

"How will you know
you're not being cheated
when it comes to money
if you can't do the numbers?"
she asks me gently.
"That's why *they* don't care
if we learn it."

At our school,
Fifina will be
doing the figures
and teaching math.

Mission School

Fifina and I
sit together at school

and listen
to Sister Gilberte,
the curly white hairs

on her chin
dancing as she talks.

I always ask her about
the country she came from.
I've decided one day
I will travel the world
with Fifina
to see "where the street
makes a corner,"
as our saying goes.

After all my questions,
one day Sister Gilberte gives in.
After class,
she shows us
a map in a book,
puts her finger on
a jagged shape
called Europe,
then points to
a tiny patch.
Her country,
Belgium.

She shows us a postcard
from her mother
of a gray land
pressed flat by low clouds.

"Those clouds are so heavy
they'll smother the fields,"
I say. "Is that why you came here?"

Would I want to leave home
if I had a chance?

Fields of Blood

"I'll tell you a story."
Sister Gilberte's big leather book
is stained and smells moldy
but she holds it open
on her lap
with the care
of a priest
holding his Bible.

"My fiancé fought
on one of those fields
in a war
they said
would end all wars.

"I went to live
in a city of women,
a béguinage
where women make laws
and decisions together.

"For hundreds of years,
they've existed.

"Walled cities were our home
when men went to war
or the Crusades.

"We took such good care
of each other

that when the men returned
many of us stayed there.

            "If we could do that then,
            we can do anything now."

She shows us
a faded photo
of a young man in a uniform,
moon face, thin lips.

"André was a university student
in Louvain,
where my father was his teacher."

"What's a university?"

"A place where
men read big books
and tell others
what's in them."

"Why only men?
Are they priests, too?"

"Let me finish my story!"

Sister Gilberte's face
moves from sunlight to cloud.

"André was a man of peace,
but he went to war
to defend our country.

"They found his body

"hanging over barbed wire
shot through with bullets.

"Our country
became Europe's battlefield,
filled with blood and bones."

She takes off her glasses
and rubs her eyes.

"Within a month,
I took my vows
to marry Christ.

"I made a choice
to leave my old life behind

"as far as I could.

"And here I am."

Her eyes are red-rimmed.

"The trouble with love
is the cracks in your heart
never mend."

She blinks fast,
bites her lip.

Can any love be worth
those tears and cracks
that nothing in the world
can ever mend?

May that love
of blood and gray clouds
of heart-burnt ashes
I've seen Papa suffer
pass me by.

Sixteen

Today Tante Lila wakes me
with my favorite breakfast,
akasan drizzled with honey,
black coffee
with brown sugar.

She kisses my cheek,
her lips cold and dry.

"Happy birthday, my niece.

"You're a woman now,
even if you don't
look like one yet."

She glances down
at my chest
and sighs.

"At your age
I was already
bleeding
and men were lined up,
begging to marry me.

"Of course those days
are long gone. And it
sure doesn't look like
those things
will ever happen to you."

This time I had to speak up
It was my birthday, after all.

"Tante Lila, are you saying
you think I'm ugly?"

"Well, you're not pretty."

Finally, she says what she thinks.

So what? I want to shout,
but instead I'm
blinking back tears.

She doesn't see me.
And I know she never will.
I decide not to care.
She's not Manman,
who I know
would never say that.

Anger tears at my appetite.

"Hurry up and finish.
Your father has a surprise."

Papa's Gift

Papa gives me
a piece of pine
the size of his palm.

He turns it
over and over.

His smile
is like the sun
breaking through clouds.

"Our eyes don't see
how wood is alive,
like water.

"Look for the shapes
that hide in the wood.

"Listen to what
the wood wants to be.
Look hard and listen
before you use your knife."

Then he gives me
my own carving knife,
like his but smaller

mother-of-pearl handle
sharp, sleek blade
gleaming in the sun.

"Thank you!"
I am dazzled by the light
on its blade.

I will sleep
with my knife

safe
under my pallet

strap it to my belt
in the leather sheath
Papa made.

My knife

will never leave me.

The First Time

My birthday afternoon
moves like thick wild honey
on manioc.

Everything slows down,
even my heartbeat.

"Happy birthday,
Ti Sè!"

Even though she can't
climb Mapou with me,
Fifina brings me gifts

from her father's office,
where he makes
his own newspaper,
and prayer cards, catechisms,
wedding invitations.

He wears thick glasses
because he reads too much.

She hands me two sheets of paper,
soft and white
flecked with wood pulp,

and a shiny orange pencil,
already sharpened,

plump eraser on its end,
smooth in my hand.

"Thank you!" I kiss
her peach-soft cheek.

Throat tight, heart pounding

the first time
I've drawn
on paper this clean
this new,
instead of with
a twig in the dirt.

I rub out my first
nervous lines.

Where do I start?

Drawing Fifina

In profile.

I start with a line
from her forehead
down along her nose
rounding her lips,
her chin and neck.

Then I fill in
her ocean of hair,
her long rope of braid.

Return to
the curve of her breasts

grown so quickly this year:
hungry glances from men
and pursed lips from women.

Her small hands
with needle and thread
stitching butterflies.

The last thing I draw
are her eyes

flickering sun
on dark water.

Cave Drawings

"Since it's my sixteenth birthday,
I'm queen for the day, right?
I can do what I want."

Fifina nods, with a smile.

"Well, I want to go
to the cave. The one your mother goes to
with the others. I think my mother went there
with yours once. Papa went, too. To hide the drums.
He said he saw drawings on the cave walls.
Messages from the first people here to us.
My mother understood what they meant.

"My father let all that slip
the night after sòlda Ameriken yo
left, when the whole village celebrated
and he joined in,
drinking too much kleren."

"You know we're not supposed to go there.
If the Sisters find out . . ."

"How will they? My lips are sealed. Please?"
I tilt my head and
clasp my hands in prayer.

"OK. Anything for my Ti Sè.
But we have to be quick.
I have to be home before dark."

We make our way
up wooded cliffs
up to the waterfall,
then take an overgrown path
hidden by broken branches.

But we're not alone.

There's a policeman from the Garde,
trained by the sòlda Ameriken yo,
who, just like our President Vincent,
hates those who serve the spirits,
thinks they are backward,
and need to convert.

He sees us
and stomps out his cigarette.

"Hey, what are you doing here?"

"We were lost," says Fifina,
trying to sound like
a lost little girl.

"Come here so I can see you
and report you to
the section chief."

We grab each other's hands and run
as fast as we can. Stones fly past our heads.
Brambles scratch our knees.

Out of danger,
we collapse in each other's arms,
breathing deep from exhaustion,
half wincing and laughing.

Fifina has one arm around me,
and with her right hand she unbuttons
just one button.
Enough for me to see
the heaving fullness of her breasts

and take it in.

She smells of pine needles and sweat,
her long loose hair tickles my face.

I brush it from my cheek
and let my hand linger on hers
for a moment.

She doesn't move away.

So I kiss her on
the side of her neck,
not the cheek, like we usually do.

She inhales softly,
her lips parted.
She doesn't pull away.

I let myself hope that,
besides our school,

there might be other things
we want to do together.

"Best birthday ever,"
I whisper.

Our goodbye hug
longer.

Even better than in my dreams.

We make it home
just before dark.

DECEMBER 15, 1935

Without Her

The first day
I thought
          her days of blood
          had come again.

The second day
I drew her face
over and over
in my notebook.

The third day
I stared out the window
and was startled
when Sister Gilberte
called on me.

The fourth day
stretched flat and gray,
like Belgian clouds.

The fifth day
Sister Gilberte
asked me to stay after class.

"Fifina isn't coming back to school.
I'm sorry. I know you were close."

Her voice is softer
than I've ever heard before.

My heart pounds so hard
I can't hear my thoughts,
tongue thick with fear.

"Why? Where is she?"

"I don't know. Her mother
would not say."

"Why would she leave
without saying goodbye?"

I try my best
to keep my tears
on the inside,
but my voice trembles.

"Is she ever coming back?"

Sister Gilberte
pulls her rosary from her pocket.

"We must pray for her.

"Her mother gave me this
for you."

A small hand-stitched book
embroidered with butterflies,
a pinkie-thin pencil,
tied with a ribbon.

Recettes lakay
pou Ti Sè.

Her mother's home recipes
just as she'd promised.

My hands shake
as I take it.

The Recipes

The title's in Kreyol,
but the recipes are in French.
Even though
she can write Kreyol
because her mother taught her,
she knows that I can't
read it very well.

She thought of it all.

Recipes for headaches and sore throats,
indigestion and asthma.

For when
my own days
of blood
pounce upon me.

For acne, dry skin,
bad breath, nails broken.

She even left
blank pages in the back
for me to write my own recipes.

*And what about
hearts broken?*

My most-needed recipe,
she didn't include.

Empty

Her place next to mine   stays empty.

Everyone else acts   like she never existed.

The sun in my heart   too sick to rise.

Fifina's Recipe

For When Your Heart Is Cracked Open

Gather all
you have
on hand,
and make sure
you see it.

Then start
to listen
with the ear
of your heart.

Breathe
deeper,
keep going.

Forget about time.

Lay your head
on me
before
falling asleep.

Famn Lakou

The best way
to find Fifina,
will be through
the famn lakou,
women who
know everything about everyone
through the teledjol grapevine.

Whenever Tante Lila
talks to the famn lakou

I crouch quiet
    out of sight
to hear all their stories.

This time
the one story I need
is Fifina's.

When I asked Tante Lila,
she just said,

"This is not a story
for ti moun."

I begged, did every chore
before she even asked,
but still she wouldn't relent.

The famn lakou,
whose voices I know well,
try to hide some stories
on the highest shelves,
way in the back.

Those are the ones
I need most.

The Outside Wife

After waiting crouched
for an hour,
I start to catch hints of Fifina's story
from the famn lakou.

"Now Fifina. That poor family.
Remember when they first
locked Mesye Schulman up?" says Tante Lila.

Fifina's father was in jail?

"How can we forget? Sòlda Ameriken yo
really hated those German Haitians.
They wanted their businesses,
and they found excuses. They accused him
of giving weapons to the Cacos,"
says the office cleaner.

"Any excuse, but he *was* on their side . . ."
the prison cleaner pipes in.

"Remember how they'd brag
about cutting off the Cacos' heads
to pass around like trophies?"
she adds.

"I heard one of them cut off
all the ears of the Cacos he'd killed
and had a necklace made
to show them all off."

Groans and heavy sighs.

"They were something else.
Dark skin, light skin,
they really didn't care about all that.

"A nèg was a nèg.

"To them, every last one of us
was a beast. A mule
they could kick
to death
if they wanted.

"So who
were the real beasts?"
The washerwoman's voice
is as heavy as her basket
of dirty sheets
from the hospital.

"We lost too many good men
and women to the Occupation.

Thank God sòlda Ameriken yo
are gone.

"Didn't they look like crabs
with their skin baked red
in our sun?"
asks the office cleaner.

A burst of laughter
before things turn serious
again.

"Even so,
their good friend
the section chief
is still here,"
says the washerwoman.

Silence.

"Did the section chief
really have a choice?"
asks Tante Lila.

"Maybe not back then,
but he does now,"
says the office cleaner.

"The first time
they arrested Mesye Schulman,
it was because he wrote
in his newspaper
about what the section chief
and the occupiers did,
grabbing all the men
who were strong enough,

throwing them in jail,
just so they could
use them like slaves
to work on their roads.

"They said he was paid
for each man he gave them.
And that's just
the beginning,"
adds the woman
who cleans the prison

ever since her husband
crossed the border
one year to cut cane
and never returned.

"*Hummph.* What's new?"
says the office cleaner.

"What was
Four-Eyes Schulman thinking?

"A cornered dog,
always shows his teeth."

The canteen cook
for the Garde d'Haiti
jumps in.

"I heard the gendarmes say
they made Mesye Schulman watch
when they smashed his printing press
and everything else
in his newspaper office.

"At gunpoint, they
told the workers to go home
and never come back.
Then they dragged him away."

The prison cleaner adds,
"I saw his wife and daughter
bring bouillon because
they knocked all his teeth out,
and of course
they smashed his glasses
and handed them to his wife."

A long sigh

and then

she adds quietly,

"I saw the section chief
staring at Fifina
at her First Communion.
We all know
how he likes them young."

Clucks of disgust.

"We all know
men like young flesh,
but this is too much!"
cries the washerwoman.

"Will those kind never let girls
just be girls? Never let them
grow into their bodies
and decide for themselves
whose touch they want?"

Her questions remain unanswered,
clouding the room like fog.

"What happened
to Mesye Schulman?"
asks the canteen cook.

"I don't know,"
says the prison cleaner.
"One day he was there.
The next day he was gone.
They told me to
clean his cell with bleach."

Someone let slip
that the section chief
promised Fifina
he'd let her father live
if she became
his outside wife.

"What choice did she have?
What would you
have done?"
asks the prison cleaner,
her voice breaking.

I close my eyes
to smother my tears.

So this was why Fifina
had never mentioned her father's arrest.
Arrested, tortured.
Now who knows
where he is?

I cover my mouth
to muffle dry retching.
No one can know
I heard all of this.

Fifina's body had bloomed
with breasts like mangoes.

Why was it her fault
that men's hungry eyes
followed her

impatient
to feast on her nectar?

Since the day she vanished
no one has told me
what happened. But tonight
I learned things the gran moun
thought we shouldn't know.

They are all wrong.
Hiding the sores
won't make them feel better.

To find Fifina,
I *will* find the section chief.

"Man proposes, Bondye disposes,"
says Tante Lila.
"The Good Lord has a plan
for us all."

Please, God,
may I never
become a woman.

Mapou's Song

Just because you've lost me doesn't mean I'm gone.
My roots are firm fingers gripping the earth.
My roots are rivers that flow underground.
My roots are an underwater forest.
In the forest, we feed each other
and talk to each other, just as I sing to you.
Keep listening. You'll know where to find me.

Those serving the spirits
know how to treat us.
We house the lwas.
Legba, Gede, Dan Petwo,
we house them and more.

We also grow near
freshwater springs,
so wherever you find us
you know you'll be safe.

It's true that it hurts
to be taken away by bandits
hacking at me in the night.
We know they did this
with the other trees.

Maybe they'll sell me over the border.
Maybe they'll build a house with me
or use the white silk around my seeds
for mattresses
or carve me into a canoe.

I hope they'll use my seeds
and sap for growing plants and healing bodies.

Only my flowers that bloomed in the night
will be lost forever.

Forever is how long
some think we live.

We remind people that time
is not measured
the small way you think it is.

That's why believers sing to us:

Rasin Mapou, ki le li ye?
Rasin Mapou, ki le li ye?
Soley leve nan Ginen.

Mapou's roots, what time is it?

The sun rises nan Ginen
home of the ancestors
underwater home to us all.

When your ancestors were brought in chains,
the first people fled higher
to the mountains hidden in clouds.

Some ran for hours
in the night and joined them.

We gave them shelter when they needed to rest.

Others stayed to fight
with machetes and torches.

We saw their blood soak the earth.

When bodies free spirits,
they return to us.

We give them a home.

I will miss the two of you,
twined orchids at my feet.

I'll show you the way
to the section chief's house,
and you'll find me there.

Don't be afraid.

Don't be frightened.

Everything is changing.

Just because you've lost me

doesn't mean I'm gone.

JANUARY 25, 1936

Dream Window

This was always
my favorite time of day,

when the world holds its breath

and the window to my night dreams

is still half open.

But last night,
I heard Mapou sing.

In this pause
of blurred soft light,
I open the bamboo gate.

Hurry down the path

        past caves where ancestors
        painted visions on grotto walls
        that we are kept from seeing

            past the waterfall
            where the gods once lived.

At the bottom of the road,
I stop to catch my breath,
        turn around,
        and hesitate.

Under the thatched roof,
Tante Lila in her room
and Papa in his,
still asleep.

The leaves of my orange tree
gleam silver in the dawn.

That same tree
Papa planted
the day I was born,
placenta buried
at its root

        for good luck.

I rush down
the wooded ravine

        across the gravel knolls
        where the hawks fly high

through the pine tree forest,
where fallen branches
crackle
under my feet.

Gone

I finally reach the spot
where I climbed Mapou's branches
with Fifina,
where I usually see
red-bottom birds,
their beaks soaked in resin.

Today
all I see
is a stump.

I fall to my knees.

A gray cloud gathers,
spreads heavy in my heart.

First Fifina, now Mapou.
I turn to the sky
and scream their names
until my voice
turns to dust.

Step Through

I run
    past the houngfor temple
        I am forbidden to enter,
           its silk flags calling
                only those who serve
                    the spirits.

Past the church
where Sister Gilberte
teaches reading, writing, and numbers

and has been praying
with me for Fifina.

When I finally reach town,
my legs are aching.
I rest for a moment
to wipe the beaded sweat
from my upper lip.
If only I could have
a sip of water first,
but the fountain
is dry.

Across the square,
schoolgirls in tidy blue uniforms
file past, neat hair
braided, in ribbons.
I want to follow *them*
instead of doing
this.

I touch my knife
for luck,

take a deep breath,
    step through the door
        of the police station

to report that someone
has stolen Mapou.

Fists

I've always had
what Tante Lila calls
"a sensitive nose."
She's annoyed
that I can smell the exact kind of wood
Papa is working on,
and she can't.

After hearing what happened
from the famn lakou,
I had nightmares
that woke me up.

Like Mapou's last song.

Fear smells
like sweat and despair.
It's mushroomed here
for years

where only one flag now stands:
Haiti's thick band of blue
above ruby-red earth,
the royal palm tree
in the center standing proud,
with gold cannons on a hill

ready to fire again,
united against invaders,
"L'Union Fait la Force."

> Sòlda Ameriken yo,
> les blans, are gone
> after nineteen years,
> tired of always fighting
> those who didn't want them.

A portrait of the section chief
next to President Vincent,
so light he looks white,
glares down at me.

People always told me
some section chiefs
were good.

But not this one

> He helped the blans.

> People who dared complain
> were taken
>> in the belly of the night

> handed over
> and sent away
> forced to build
> the road from our capital
> to Cap-Haïtien,
> the city prezidan Roosevelt
> visited to admire
> all the friendliness
> his army had spread.

Those were the lucky ones.

Others died in misery,
covered with bruises, open wounds,
bones and spirits broken

or just vanished
        like Fifina
        and her father.

Lives emptied like pockets,
families praying, begging
        for news,
                remains,
                        anything at all

they could bury.

Now that I know all this,
my heart is a tight fist.

La Corvée

In the police station,
fear chokes my heart
as it did only once before.

A memory I buried so deep
comes rising up
like bile in my throat.

I was walking with Tante Lila
back from church,
holding her hand,
barely reaching her hips.
Was I three or four?

Then came a man,
fish-belly white
on a proud black horse,
and behind him
men roped together
as if they were chained.

        Mountain vultures drew   eager circles

                overhead.

Everyone else on the road
        stopped.
Some looked down;
some turned away.

Tante Lila pulled me close
to cover my eyes,
but I wriggled free.

The men were mainly dressed alike,
in faded gray-and-white stripes.
The youngest had
blood crusting his lips,
right eye swollen shut,
left eye filled with emptiness
like trudging mules
chained to the millstone.

"What did those men do?"
I asked Tante Lila.

She frowned.
Put her finger to her lips.

Only when the last guard
disappeared down the road
did she speak.

> "Poor souls.
> They are prisoners, going to build
> roads for les blans."

> > "Are they zonbis?"

> "Ma fille, such questions
> are not for ti moun.

> "Short legs should walk faster
> to get home before dark."

Stolen

I grip the counter
to stop myself shaking.

> "I want to report
> something stolen."

My voice echoes loudly
in this quiet room
except for the creaky fan,
watching from above.

The young officer,
crisp in khaki,
barely inches
his newspaper down.
"The lost and found
is closed today."

He doesn't bother
to cover his mouth
when he yawns loud and slow
and returns to his newspaper.

I stand and wait.

After a few minutes,
the gendarme,
trained by the blans,
looks up at me
and sighs.

He flicks me
a faded yellow form,
thin brittle paper
that might crumble
in my fingers.

I write carefully
with the pretty neat loops
Sister Gilberte taught me

then hand it back
and watch
him: eyebrows raised,
lips moving.

> "I see. *Your* mapou
> is missing
> and you know
> exactly who took it.
> Are you sure your tree
> didn't go for a walk?"

He leans back in his chair,
tenting the newspaper over his knees.

I say,
    "I know exactly where it is."

When Mapou sings,
I don't need a map.

I step away from the counter,
praying he will follow.

Sweat

I nudge past
a small group
that has gathered,
their curious stares
now challenging him.

The wild-honey woman
setting up her stall on the square
speaks without looking up.

"Are you really too busy
to help this poor girl
from the Mission School?
We don't pay taxes
so you can sit all day
and read the papers!"

The crowd sniggers,
all eyes on him.

He breathes heavy behind me.
His sweat smells
like curdled milk.

We trudge in silence
until we reach
the front gate
of a new concrete house.

I stop
and take a deep breath:
it was exactly like this
in Mapou's song,
even the white lace curtains.

The policeman stops and turns to me.

"But this—this is
the section chief's house,"
he says, mopping the sweat
from his neck
with a damp handkerchief.

"The section chief
is supposed to help
all those who ask,"
says a market woman
balancing a papaya-filled basket
on her head.
"So go get his help!"

The gendarme knocks slowly.

No sign of anyone home.
Then the lace curtain

in the second-floor window
shifts.

A servant appears at the door.

"Monsieur is away in the capital
on *official* business,"
she says, disdain in her voice,
her eyes sweeping the crowd.

The lace curtain closes.

Found

I reach over
the acacia thorn fence
to point out
a pile of mapou trees
sawed down
stacked high

my mouth dry
when I speak.

"That's the one."
I point ahead.

He pulls down
his broad-brimmed hat
to cover more of his face.

"How can you tell?"

"Why would she lie?"
says the market woman,
putting down her basket.

The crowd that has gathered
murmurs in agreement.

I close my eyes.

> *I know my Mapou.*
> *I held her close.*
> *I felt her breathing.*
> *I've drawn her*
> *over and over*
> *in the earth.*

The crowd grows larger.

A second market woman
flips over
her empty basket
to sit and watch,
chin in hand.

> "Euh. It's about time
> that *one* of you does something.
>
> "We all saw the blans
> with the help of the Church
> cut down our trees,
> to stop those
> who serve the spirits.
>
> "But you should know
> bad things happen
> to those who cut down
> our mapous
> even if it's not
> an *official* crime."

Chortles rise
like bubbles
in a simmering pot.

The gendarme fumbles with the gate
and unlatches it.

I watch
as he bends,
peers at chopped trees.
After a few minutes,
he straightens,
clears his throat.

"I will write a report."

One long stare at me

before he hurries away.

Exhaling

The crowd

exhales

in relief and surprise

circles me

congratulates me.

The market woman
pats my shoulder.

"Brave girl!
Not many your age
would stand up like that

and do the right thing.
Your parents
should be proud."

A graying man pushes forward
to face me.

"Brave or foolish?
You've just made
the section chief your enemy.
Now you'll have to watch your back
as long as you live."

Another market woman glares at him
and hands me a ripe mango.

"Konpè, I respect you as my elder,
but please don't make fear her master.

"We need more courage in our young ones,
before life breaks them down."

I hardly hear their argument

as sweet mango juice sticks to my lips

and flows through me

like the sap of a tree.

Still Lost

When I was at
the section chief's house

I wanted Fifina's hand
to be the one
pulling back the curtains.

I wanted her to see me,
come out,

and escape.

But I knew from Mapou's song
that she wasn't there

even though
she was stolen, too.

Stolen
by the section chief
to be his "outside wife."

His mother wouldn't want Fifina
as her son's official wife.
Even with her light skin
and silky hair, she'd always be
the daughter of a Boche
who helped the Cacos.
That would not help him
climb the ranks in the army.

Mapou led me here.

I pray another dream
will lead me to her.

Tangled

The sun is still high.
Tante Lila and Papa
will be happy.

I see them
at the gate.

I'm home
before dark.

Tante Lila comes running,
hugs me tight,
pushes me away,
and slaps me.

Nettles sting my cheek.
I sniffle. Too dazed to cry.

> "What *possessed* you?
> Do you realize the section chief's *mother* was there?
> She *saw* you!
> Do you *know* what you've done?"

Once we're inside, Papa sits
at the head of the table,
his face a pine mask.

> "Have some bouillon,
> then go to bed."

How did everything go so wrong
when I did the right thing?

I don't know what they're saying,
hear only tangled voices

low and breaking,
then silence.

Even the night sounds
of crickets and tree frogs
are tangled.

Morning

This morning
each spoonful of akasan,
which I usually only get
for my birthday,
is hard to swallow.

Papa and Tante Lila
sit still, watching me eat.

Papa speaks first.

"I can't keep you safe here.
The section chief
and his mother will never forget.
They will make you pay
for revealing the truth:
they are rotten to the core.
They take whatever they want.
Their greed has swallowed their hearts.
We could all be arrested—
or worse."

He speaks slowly,
stones in his throat.

Does Papa even know about Fifina
like Tante Lila does?

"We have decided.
You will go work
for Madame Ovide.
She is someone from
une grande famille,
and her home
is where your cousin Phebus
learned to cook.
Madame Ovide will pay you and send the money
you make to me."

"Why?"

"Because that's what women do,"
says Tante Lila.

"I meant why Madame Ovide?"

Papa clears his throat.

"Your mother and Fifina's mother
were like sisters. They once helped
Madame Ovide when she was younger.
That's all you need to know."

"Your cousin Phebus
has only good things to say about her.
And you leave us no choice,"
he continues.

No choice. No more school.
No more hushed afternoons
tracing looped letters
in sky-blue notebooks.

"You will be treated well,"
says Papa.

"These sandals were your mother's.
You'll need them
in the city."

Soft smooth cowhide
with polished braided straps to circle my ankles.
He must have saved them
thinking I'd grow into them
one day.
But not for this.

I step into them.
They fit me perfectly.

"Thank you, Papa.
They are beautiful."
I kiss his cheek.
"Do I really have to go?
I promise to be good from now on."

Tante Lila throws up her hands.
Papa sighs, looks down at the sandals.

"It's too late now! The vengeance
of the section chief and his mother
is dangerous enough.
Fifina learned the hard way,
thanks to her father.

"But the section chief's mother,
they say she's a manbo
who knows
the Dark Arts."

Tante Lila grips her rosary
so hard,
I'm afraid
the beads will break.

"You leave tomorrow morning.
Don't even think
of sticking your nose
out of the house before then.
I'll pack what you need."

What I need
can't go in a suitcase.

Dark Butterfly

Tante Lila and Papa
hug me goodbye.

I've never seen
Papa cry before.

Don't want him
to let go
yet.

Papa hands me
a small leather suitcase.

"This was your mother's."

It is shut tight
with rope.

"I packed your Sunday dress
and a calico,"

says Tante Lila.
"Madame Ovide
will give you a uniform."

A uniform? Am I going
into the army?

"I can't send you letters
because I know
they'll be opened
and the police
will read what we write," says Papa.

"But I will send you
a small piece of wood
from whatever I am carving.

"You will know
I am thinking of you.

"Bon kouraj."

Behind the weathered pine
mask of Papa's face,
his eyes scan the horizon

as if courage were like
our black butterflies

that fly in the dark
toward the light.
But instead of being burned,
are filled with more life.

Flowers in Ashes

I step onto the bus,
named Bondye Si Bon,
another twist of the knife.

If God is so good
then why turn me into
a girl in the shadows

at Madame Ovide's?

> *Don't ask questions.*
> *Work in silence.*
> *Look down when spoken to.*

I repeat Tante Lila's instructions
like the Credo at Mass

fold myself
on the bench in the back
by the window.
An old woman smoking a cob pipe
squeezes next to me,
strokes the beard
of the gray goat on her lap.

The goat looks up at her
with soft trusting eyes,
no idea how near death is.

"His name is Simalo."
She offers me a piece of sugarcane.

Even if sweetness
feels wrong this morning,

refusing would be rude.
"Mèsi, ma kòmè."

I try not to cough from the pipe smoke,
strain my neck
to the gap in the window,
heart thumping in my ears.

Maybe this is a good thing.
Maybe I'll find Fifina
somewhere in the city.
Maybe that's where
the section chief keeps her.

Each village   a bumpy blur   a reminder
this is the first time
I'm this far from home.

Children playing
by the side of the road
wave and smile,
the way I used to do.
I can't wave back.

Bondye Si Bon
slows   to   a   crawl,
leaning right on the stone-filled road.

Down below the rocky cliff,
a burnt-out skeleton
of a brother bus.

Dizzy, stomach dropping,
I stare hard at the wreck,
wild mountain flowers
sprouting from its ashes.

What if I'd been sitting on that bus
when it fell to its grave?
In a second, the valley
a clenched fist.

> No time to pray
> when luck runs out
> so fast.

I squeeze my eyes shut
to stop the tears.

Cousin Phebus

Cousin Phebus will meet me
at the station.

Cousin Phebus who
stands tall like an African queen
with her ebony skin and
sparkling eyes

who taught me
to make dous lèt
while making me laugh
with her stories of
Madame Ovide and her rich ladies
wearing their white gloves and hats
and stockings,
talking about how to improve
the lives of Haitian women.

Not *all* of them are light-skinned
like Madame Ovide,
Cousin Phebus explained.

There are people
like the famous professor
Jean Price-Mars
who prove that a fine education
and a fine family
count for more.
Class is king.

The worst insult
is to call someone
a blan mannan,
those white pirates
and outlaws
no one respects.

Do Madame Ovide and her friends
really know how most of us live?
Girls like me, Fifina, and Phebus
might as well be planets in the sky
we are so far apart from them.

On the other hand,
Cousin Phebus said
they write their own magazine,
La Voix des Femmes,
so perhaps they really do care
about women's voices.

One of their magazines
was even closed down
by the government,
which means they must
be doing something right!

And if they care about
our education,
they might help me
and Fifina
start our school.

I let myself
feel that small ray of hope
before it vanishes
behind a gray cloud.

Madame Ovide

"She's not that bad,"
Cousin Phebus told me
two years ago,
the first time
she returned from the city.

"Even if sometimes
she loves attention.

"Madame's husband,
now dead,
was an ambassador
so famous
his family
appears on stamps.
They own land
and houses all over
the country."

How does it feel
to see your face on a stamp?

Moun

A jolt from the bumpy road
brings me back
from the edge of sleep.

Electric streetlamps glow
bright in Port-au-Prince,
but beyond them it's nearly dark.

Men in white jackets with gleaming canes
and women in high heels
(some even in pants!),
their lips painted,
parade along a wide road.

Phebus was right about
seeing every color
under the sun.
I remember the time she wrote down
all the categories
made by the French
before we freed ourselves,
based on how much black blood we had.

The numbers meant nothing to me,
but we still use their labels:
sacatra, griffe, marabou, mulâtre,
quarteron, metis, mamelouk,
quarteronné, sang-mêlé.

Of course to the sòlda Ameriken yo,
we were all lumped in one pile.
When people like the Ovides
realized this, and felt the sting of losing
their rank and status,

unity became more important
than all the categories.

We all understood that
being a mulâtre, like being a blan,
was about much more than color.
After all, "blan"
means a foreigner
of any color.

"Tout moun se moun,"
says our proverb.
Every person
is a person.

It was *us* against *them*.

Stones in the Sun

A band of gleaming brass
plays marching tunes
beneath the gazebo.

"This is the Champ de Mars,"
says the goat lady,
tugging gently at Simalo's beard.

I twist in my seat
to take in every sight.
At least the market women
look like the ones back home.
One taps on my open window,
trying for a last sale,

but the bananas and papayas
here look smaller and paler.

The market woman holds up
a paper cone of roasted peanuts
that smell so good
I'm tempted to spend
the centimes Papa gave me.

This is the time of day
I'd say goodbye
to Mapou,
put down the pine
I was carving,
and go home to eat.

My stomach growls.

I can smell goat meat grilling
in our courtyard.

I can see Tante Lila
shaping the flour
for cloud dumplings.

I'll show them all.

I'll find Fifina
and bring her back,
no matter how long it takes.

I found Mapou, after all.

I can dream
the truth
again.

Bondye Si Bon groans to a stop
at the end of the road.
The woman with the goat moves
him from her lap.
He stands up, wobbling
like a child learning to walk.

She grips the rope
around his neck
with knotted fingers,
steadies herself
on my shoulder,
and leans in close.

"Country, city,
where the street
makes a corner.
It doesn't matter
where you go.

"Stones in the water
don't know the pain
of stones in the sun."

She waves goodbye,
pauses, and sighs,
then walks away slowly
from Bondye Si Bon.

PART TWO
LAVIL

Dry Twigs

At the bus terminal,
the streetlamp glows
on a thin woman
with sad eyes.

That can't be Cousin Phebus.

It's true she hasn't been home
for Christmas in a few years,
but still, I'm surprised
to see how much she's changed.
"Ti Cousine! Don't tell me
you've forgotten
your favorite cousin!"
the thin woman says.

Her little laugh
sounds like dry twigs
snapping.

Cousin Phebus,

      who used to swing me   in circles

until my feet

      flew   high   off   the   ground.

*Why does a cook
look like she's starving?*

Behind her smile,
a sadness.

She takes my hand
and my small suitcase,

tries not to grin
at the rope.

"You're so lucky
to work for Madame Ovide,"
says Cousin Phebus.

Together we walk
on the Chemin des Dalles
to Bois Verna,
where the houses
are like castles
carved with
towers and balconies,
set back from the street
enough to be admired
but with gates
to keep people out.

My heart skips a beat
with excitement at the
fairy-tale houses,
with their delicate carved wood lattices.
My first time in the capital
feels like a daydream.

Papa would love these.

On Cousin Phebus's palm
I feel a scar, a rocky island
of flesh.

"Did you burn yourself
when you were cooking?"

Cousin Phebus
pulls away her hand.

We walk on in silence.

Tree frogs croak high
in the thick night air.

"We both
have our secrets to keep.

"I heard what you did.
Weren't you afraid?"

"No," I lie.

"You should be.
The section chief's mother
has an elephant's memory."

I remember the shadow
behind the lace curtain
when the policeman knocked.

"I still want to go home."

Cousin Phebus turns
to face me.

"Don't you even *know*
how lucky you are?"

This time her voice
is on fire with anger
and pain.

I know I'm lucky
compared to Fifina and her family,

Sister Gilberte's fiancé,
the boys and men in chains.

"It's just that
I want to
run my own school
like Sister Gilberte—"

"You think that will happen now?
I thought you were *smart*."

We reach the gate
of a blue-and-white mansion,
a castle in the sky.
The most beautiful house
I've ever seen.

"This is Madame Ovide's."
Cousin Phebus's hand
trembles,
clammy in mine.
She pulls it away
and points around the back.

Why is she shaking like this?
I thought she liked
working here.

"Go through
the courtyard
to that little house
in the back.
You'll see
where you'll sleep."

She rings the bell.

"Don't go off
by yourself
and do something stupid
again," she adds softly.
"The tallest tree
is always chopped down first."

Shadow Girl

The yard boy meets me
at the gate. Brings me inside
by a side door, in the part of the house
where the servants live.

Where I now live.

At least I have my own room.

My first night
sleeping away from home.

Itchy rag-stuffed mattress
bumpy on my back,
not like my smooth straw mat
back home.

I toss and turn
on my bed of thorns,
questions tormenting me
like bedbugs.

*What happened
to Fifina?
What happened
to my cousin?*

What will happen
to me?

What if Cousin Phebus is right
and what I did was stupid?

I'm a mountain
emptied out.

I miss:

Papa   Fifina   Sister Gilberte

Mapou

Even Tante Lila

making me wince
when she washed and untangled
my thick bushy hair,
telling me to stop squirming,
smoothing castor oil
onto my scalp
as I sat on the floor
between her knees.

Even that,
I'll miss.

The classroom smell   of soft white chalk   on gray slate.

Cracked leather books   Sister Gilberte opened
when the cracks in her heart   grew too wide.

Papa polishing my carving   handing it back
with two words I loved: "Well done."

Fifina's neck   misted with sweat when I kissed it.

Mapou's leaves   that danced   when I touched them.

The window   to my dreams

now closed.

Country Girl

I turn over again
on the mattress,
feel its resistance
against my back.

Even the night sounds here
are not like home,
where frogs and crickets
sing together.

Here the tree frogs croak
thin and high.

The crickets don't respond.

I try to picture
the woman who owns all this,
but my mind refuses.

What I want right now
is to run
all the way home.

Morning

When I hear
the pipirit's song
of dawn

I get up,
wash my face,
feet, hands
with the courtyard pump.

I step into the sandals Papa made,
remember his face
when he gave them to me.

The gray uniform
draped over an old
cane-and-straw chair
is stiff. Too big
for me
in the chest and hips.

Another girl's body
molded its shape.
Another girl's sweat
darkened its armpits.

My arms and legs
are twigs
trapped in gray.
I tie the white apron
twice around my waist.

A tall round woman
who looks as old as Tante Lila
comes out from

one of the other rooms.
Gray hair peeps from
beneath her madras headwrap,
but her face is smoother
than Sister Gilberte's.

The houseboy
joins her
and makes us all
sweet black coffee.

"I'm Celestina," the woman says.
"Been working here
since I was a girl.
And you must be Lucille."

I nod.

"A real country girl
is always up
before the sun."

I'm not sure
if I've already made
a mistake
my very first day
at Madame Ovide's.

We finish our coffee
squatting in front of
an open-sided building
where I see chicken feathers
on the table.

Celestina sprinkles
a few drops from

the bottom of the cup
on the ground—
"for the ancestors,"
she says.

She walks us over
to the open building.
"The real kitchen is inside,
but we pluck the chickens
and gut the fish out here.
Can you cook
like your cousin?"

I nod
and stare at the long charcoal stove,
cast-iron pots and pans,
lined up neatly.

"Here is the icebox.
Only I can open it."
She points to the key
around her neck.

"You can start
by shelling peas
soaking beans
pounding millet
plucking and skinning.
You've done all that before, right?"

"I used to help Cousin Phebus
before she came here,
before I went to school."

"Euh, you went to school?
Then why are you here?"

I hesitate.

"My father is ill. My aunt
is caring for him.
I'm working here
until he gets better.
Then I'll go home."

My lie feels better
than explaining
the truth.

Finding Fifina

I unfold my drawing of Fifina.

"Have you seen my friend?
She went missing
from my village."

Celestina squints,
sighing as she shakes her head.

"Such a pretty girl.
If she's in the city, I hope
she's not on her own.

"Bad things happen
to girls on their own."

She takes another look
before moving me along.

"May Bondye protect her.

"Come on, now. There's more to show you
before you start working."

I turn away
so Celestina won't see
the tears brimming.

Butterfly World

We walk quickly
through the courtyard

and enter paradise.

Deep-pink bougainvillea
on trumpet vine
curls over the garden wall,
spider lilies, white oleander,
blood-red hibiscus

sharp lemon-tree scent
mingles with jasmine,
ylang-ylang, gardenia.

Butterflies flutter
from color to color.

At the center
a marble fountain,
chubby angel spouting
water from its mouth.

A standing parasol
like a soft white cloud
shades the table
and four wrought-iron chairs.

*What is it like to live
each day in paradise?*

Work

Celestina doesn't linger long.
Our day's work is waiting.

"My cousin Paul
is the driver. My cousin Dieudonné
is the gardener. His son is my godson,
Felix, the yard boy.

"There are other servants
that come and go
for parties and dinners,
but they don't live with us.

"Madame Ovide is from
a place called Cazales.
She told me all the people
look like her
and used to speak a strange language
and came from far away.

"Madame only comes outside
when the sun isn't too bright.
Truth is,
she doesn't want the sun
to ruin her light skin."

She eyes me sideways.

"At least we'll never have that problem!"

For the first time
since leaving home

I smile.

Celestina's joke,
so many flowers in one place
butterflies fluttering
and that angel
whose trickling water
reminds me
of the waterfall
near my village.

"Come on, country girl."
Her voice is gentler.

"We can't afford
to waste time."

Crystal Waterfall

From the garden,
we enter French doors
to a room
as large as a church.

> "This is where
> we serve the meals.
> Over there
> is the parlor."

A crystal waterfall
hangs from the ceiling,
double rainbows dancing
in the early-morning light.

My neck grows stiff
from looking up so much.

"I'd never seen one either.
It's called a chandelier.
It's made of glass.
Keeping it clean
will be your job
one day."

A long oval table
is already dressed
in lace and starched white linen
polished silver
blue-and-white china,
and blazing birds-of-paradise
in a carved crystal vase.

Madame Ovide's table
is an altar.

Even Sister Gilberte
would be speechless.

Real Shoes

Celestina nudges me along.

"Don't worry about leaving marks
on the tiles here. The yard boy
mops the floors in the morning.
I will have a seamstress
make your uniform fit,
and I will get you
some real shoes."

Real shoes?

I've heard
city people make fun
of country people
for having big feet

because we're always barefoot.

But I've always loved feeling
dirt between my toes
and the way the earth
breathes.

I glance down
at Celestina's rubber sandals.

Manman's sandals, the ones Papa gave me,
look more comfortable,
and beautiful.

I ball up my fists
to keep myself silent.

Temptation

I step carefully
through the living room,
into a room made of glass
where a black piano gleams.

I want to reach out
and touch it.

"Her only child,
Mesye Oreste,
plays like the angel
he is. I saw that boy born

94

with a caul on his head.
That's rare, you know.
It's a good sign.

"I'm the one
who wiped his bottom,
taught him his first words,
and held him tight
when his father died.
He was only ten
when his father died
of a heart attack.
We were living in Brussels.
That's the capital of Belgium,
where his father was ambassador."

That very same Belgium
where Sister Gilberte came from
and lost her one and only love.

"Mesye Oreste always called me Bébelle.
Said it was short for Bellestina,
because I was so beautiful.
When he was seven,
he said he'd marry me
one day.
Can you imagine?"

She makes a small laugh
that sounds mixed with sadness.

"That boy is my heart.

"Bondye never blessed me
with children of my own."

Like Tante Lila.

It's hard to listen
when I can't stop staring
at the piano's gleaming wood.

"You'll dust and polish.

"Except for the piano. You are
never to touch it.

"I will take care of it,
like I always have.

"I'll show you how to set the table.

"The bedrooms are upstairs.

"When Madame is out,
I'll show you how to make a bed.

"Don't make any noise
while she's asleep."

That piano's glowing wood
reminds me of Mapou.

Maybe one day
it will sing to me,
just like Mapou.

A music book waits open
on the piano.

The magic of sounds
from signs on paper
that look like
the black footprints
of birds.

The Queen and Her Prince

The silver-framed
photo on the piano
shows a light-skinned woman
seated like a queen
with her little prince.

"That's Mesye Oreste."
A frail-looking boy,
light curls caressing
his forehead,
with the pouty lips of a girl,
stands with his hands
on his mother's shoulders.

"He'll be back next week
from a trip to Paris,"
she says smiling.

"Always brings me something
wherever he travels.
I remember
helping him
take his first steps.
He was so proud
and looked up at me
as if to say, 'Look, Bébelle!
Look what I can do!'"

She tilts her head
and picks up the photo,
gazing. "I watched him grow
from a boy to a young man."
Her smile turns to me.

"How old are you?"
she asks.

"Sixteen."

"*Hummph.*
You look younger,
flat as a board.
With that fuzz on your lip,
you look like a boy.

"At your age,
I had curves
that stopped men
dead in their tracks."

*I've heard this before,
from Tante Lila.*

*Why do some women need to tell me
how much they were wanted by men?*

"Even the ambassador
flirted with me
when Madame
wasn't around.
He said I was
the real salt of the earth.

"Had a lot of proposals
and turned them all down.
Why let some man
tell me what to do?

"*This* is my family."

Her sad-smile laugh.

Celestina sighs
and crosses her arms.
"Anyway, that was then."

"As for you, I can't imagine
any man will bother."

> Like they bothered with
> Fifina? God help any man who tries.

I feel for my knife
strapped under my skirt.

Meeting the Queen

When Madame Ovide
finishes her breakfast in bed,
she calls for me.
"You arrived late last night."

"I'm sorry . . . Madame."
I'll need to remember
to always say Madame.

Madame presses her lips
to a starched white napkin.
I try not to stare.

I never knew women
wore lipstick in bed.

Today is a day
filled with firsts.

I can always tell
a woman's age

by the lines in her neck,
like the rings of a tree.
Madame's are light creases.
She's much younger than Tante Lila
and Fifina's mother.
In fact,
she doesn't look old enough
to have a son as tall
as Oreste.

The china plate
on Madame's tray
holds two slices of
a strange red fruit
with dark seeds
scooped to the side.

The red of her nails
is like the red of her lips.

"How's your cousin?
She told me she likes
her job cooking
for Madame Perez."

"She's very well, thank you."

I remain standing by the bed,
hands clasped behind my back
head slightly bowed
to better peek
at Madame Ovide
without getting caught.

Plump and light-skinned,
straight nose,
soft wavy hair
in a tight chignon
the color of wet sand.

Cheve swa, like Fifina.

Not like mine
so wild and puffy
Tante Lila had to wrestle
and yank it
into cornrows so tight
they pulled at my face.

Now I can cut my hair
as short as I want.

Stay in Your Place

Madame peers over
her coffee cup.
"Come closer."

She holds my face
in her hands. "Your father
and cousin say you're a good girl."

I have no idea
if I should respond
or stay silent.

Up close, Madame's eyes
are jewels of green and gold,

like the eyes of the gray cat
in the churchyard.

"Were you baptized?"

"Yes, Madame. I even
received my First Communion
when I studied with the Sisters."

She lets go
of my face, her fingers
cool and soft.

I've already talked too much.
Staying quiet will be hard to learn.

"Your cousin
tells me you can read and write."

She pauses, looks down
at my sandals.

I straighten my back.

"What else can you do?"

>   *Does she know*
>   *about the section chief?*

"I can do
anything.
I learn fast, Madame."

"We'll see. I can tell by your eyes
that you're smart.
And your French is very good
for a country girl."

Her bracelet
jangles gold charms,
sparkling little suns.

"No Kreyol in the house.
My son will try to speak it with you.
Just ignore him.

"Stay in your place
and all will be fine."

Girl

Pick pluck shell wash
wipe dust polish set.

Make breakfast.
Make beds.

Set laundry
in courtyard
for washerwoman
to pick up.

Get back to kitchen.
Make the next meal.

Cook and clean
clean and cook
dust and polish.

Mind the silver!
If even one teaspoon goes missing,
you're out the door.

No need to tell me
anything twice.

Time is Master now.

Nights
so tired

even my dreams
need a nap.

Scraps

In my dream,
Fifina is pounding
a paste with mortar and pestle
and drenched in sweat.

Where is she?

I don't know.
It's not a place
I've ever seen.

She doesn't look at me.
Only says:
"Use whatever you have
on hand."

All day I wonder
what the dream means.

Then, clearing the dishes,
I see two black olives,
unwanted.

"Celestina, can I
take these scraps?"

"As long as
everyone's fed,"
she says with a shrug.

My First Recipe

Use
what you have on hand.

Take some of the vinegar.

Squeeze the juice of a lemon.

Mash up the olives
with the mortar and pestle.

Strain the olive oil
until you have enough
to make up your mixture.

Strain it through
a cheesecloth
until the drops that come out
are smooth.

My Polish

The next morning,
I wake up at four,
when workers
go to Mass,
to try out my dream.

I write down each step
I remember from my dream
and then do exactly
as my recipe says.

I clean a small empty jar
of Madame's confiture
until it is spotless.

I pour in
my new polish
as golden
as honey.

On a piece of pine
I was carving for practice
I rub my polish.

Beautiful!

I tiptoe to the piano
to try my polish
there.

"Stop!"

Celestina snatches
the cloth from my hand.

"What are you doing?"

"I—I made this wood polish,
and I thought
for the piano—"

"I told you
never to touch it!"

"But I just,
I just thought—"

"Stop thinking and just do
what I tell you to do.

"Did you ever even see a piano
in your little country village?"

I look down,
my feet ugly
in black rubber sandals.

I didn't think
she'd be this mad.
Is it just because
it's her Oreste's piano?

"Then how would you know
how to take care of one?"

My cheeks burn red.

"But—but I thought—"
I've never heard myself
stutter before.

"Stop *thinking*
you know
things you don't know.

"You have no idea
what you almost did.

"The ambassador bought this piano
in Brussels for Oreste's seventh birthday.
Oreste would be heartbroken
if anything happened to it.

107

"It should never
be polished, just dusted.

"And only *I*
will do that."

"But
you never said—"

"Never said what?
I told you *never* to touch it!"

She glares at me,
her eyes a locked icebox.

"Go outside now.
I'll bring some guinea fowl
for you to pluck."

I return to the courtyard,
rubber sandals
dragging.

Burning

Nobody wants
a troublemaker in the house,
a girl
who doesn't know her place.

Nobody wants
a country girl,
a shadow girl,
a mule.

Nobody wants
a girl
who thinks she dreams
the truth.

What if Celestina
tells Madame about the piano?

Will she
send me away?

A week of no dreams,
no drawing,
no wood to carve.

My heart
is roped tight.

Before falling asleep,
I place Fifina's butterfly book
like a pillow
beneath my head

to invite my dreams
back.

Cedar

Celestina keeps me
in the courtyard
plucking fowl
soaking beans
stirring soup
peeling lemons
scrubbing pots.

Today Cousin Phebus came by
to give me a package from Papa:
a small piece of cedar
whose rich scent I inhaled
to fill up the emptiness.

Is this simply
a precious gift from Papa,
or is it a message?

People like their coffins
made from cedar:
it protects them
from evil
and becoming zonbis.

"Is Papa
in danger?"

"He's fine—don't you worry.
We're making a plan."

Cousin Phebus says she likes
working for Jeanne Perez
and the ladies from La Ligue.

"Jeanne didn't grow up
wearing white gloves.
She was born like us,
and raised by her
mother and sister.
She's one of us,
but the white-gloved ladies
respect her.

"When Jeanne writes,
she asks my opinion.
She gives me each issue
of her magazine to read
and keep. I'm learning more
than I ever did back home."

Not quite like me.

But I'm happy for her.

When Madame sends the money
to Papa,
I could add a note
for the town scribe
to read to him.

But what if someone else reads it,
and tells the section chief where I am?

I could write to
Sister Gilberte.

But what if someone asks her
where I am?
She said lying is a sin.

Would she lie for me?

Where else can I go
when I can't go home?

Glow

Celestina is still angry
with me
for daring to touch
Oreste's piano.

But still I don't believe
my dream was wrong.

I try my polish on my carvings,
see how bright they glow.

"Can I come with you
to the market?"
I finally ask Celestina
after giving her a week
to calm down.

Cousin Phebus has always said
that the Iron Market
in Port-au-Prince
is the biggest market
in the country.

I've wanted to see it
since I was a girl.

"If I can sell
this wood polish I made,
or my carving,
I'll give you half."

Celestina narrows her eyes
before she agrees.

"You're not as useless
as I thought."

Iron Market

The next morning
we leave by car
to beat the morning heat
and buy the freshest fish.

Riding in
Madame's big fancy car
is just like a dream

of smooth-water sailing,
even if,
on the capital's Grand Rue,
the ride can get choppy.

Celestina sits in the front
with Paul, the driver.

From the back seat,
I can see
the two white-capped towers
of the Iron Market
rising up from the city.
On one tower,
the word PEACE.
On the other,
WORK.

Above them, joining the two,
is the name of President Hyppolite,
with the year 1889.

If Fifina were here,
she'd quickly tell me
how many years ago that was.
All I know
is it was before the Occupation.
I stare up in awe.

As I step out of the car,
the smell hits me first,
a forceful wave of sweat,
fish, fruit, and dust.

On either side of us,
stalls filled with clothes
and other dry goods.

A man brushes past me,
ten straw hats balanced on his head,
carrying two more stacks in his hands.
Another man, covered in straw mats,
weaves quickly and easily
through narrow aisles,
even with his face nearly covered.

The man behind him
almost knocks me down
with his load of plantains.

A woman elbows her way,
carrying five live chickens
on her strong shoulders.

The energy of this place
sends sparks through my hair.

May this be
how I find my way back
to Fifina.

Madan Sara

Celestina is looking
for a market woman
she knows well
who sells wood carvings
to tourists.

Les blans.
"Not as many,
but still enough
to make money for hotel bellboys
who send them to see
'real voodoo.'" She laughs.

"She might use
your polish and
sell it herself,"
says Celestina.

Squeezing through the crowd,
we finally find her stall,
crammed with wood platters,
carved boxes, smooth bowls,
and wood sculptures
of women carrying
straw baskets on their heads.

"Do you sell voodoo dolls?"
asks a plump white man in

a damp hat and shorts.
The market woman
sizes him up.
"No, I don't, but this will make you
irresistible to the ladies."

She hands him a wood carving
of a man and woman,
legs wrapped around each other.

"Combien?"
he asks, fumbling for his wallet.

"For such a handsome gentleman,
I'll make a special price.
Just five."

"Five dollars?"
The man shakes his head.
"I'll give you one."

She folds her arms
and looks him straight in the eye.
"We can both be happy at three."

The market woman shakes his hand,
and as she wraps his carving in old newspaper
he says, "Tonight I'm going to see a voodoo ceremony.
I hope it's just like that movie
White Zombie! Have you ever seen one?
I mean, a real zombie?"

The market woman sighs
and shakes her head,
almost nudging him along
when she hands him his package.

Celestina was right.
Those kind of tourists
won't stay away.

"Bonjou, Madan Sara.
This is the new girl
at Madame Ovide's.
She has something
to show you."

Madan Sara,
hands on hips,
looks me up and down.

"Which one do you want?
You can pay in gourdes.
I always make the Ameriken
pay in dollars. That's five gourdes
for each dollar, but three
dollars sounds better to them
than fifteen gourdes!"

"No, I'm here to
ask for your help
to sell something
I made."

"Well, hurry up.
I don't make any money
using my eyeballs."

I pull out my jar
and open it.
"It's a polish I made
for wood."

I hold it up
to Madan Sara's nose.

"*Humph*. It doesn't
smell too bad."

She takes my jar,
dips a strip of calico
into the polish,
and picks up
a sculpture.

A mother and child,
not "well done,"
as Papa would say.
Heads too large,
faces too blank.

The carver was rushed
or just didn't care.

> *Next time, I'll show you*
> *what I can make.*

She gently rubs
the sculpture
with my polish.

Now
the wood is alive again,
almost breathing.
Her own reflection
glows back.

"That's not bad
for a country girl."

We shake hands.

Who knows what Madan Sara
will ask for my polish?
Whatever the blan
is willing to pay.

That's how it works
at the Iron Market.

Madan Sara tells me
she'll put my polish
in smaller jars
she can get for me.

My first try that night
had been a test,
and since then I'd been making
more every day.

For every jar she sells,
she will pay
me some money.

Celestina adds that
she will get half
for introducing us.

"That's how it works,"
she says.

So I won't get much,
but it will add up.

"Little by little,
the bird builds its nest,"

says the proverb. Papa
likes that one.

"Can you get me
some wood
so I can make my own carvings
and see if they sell?
I have some small pieces
from my father,
but I will need more."

Madan Sara
puts her hands on her hips.

"Well, well, well.
You've got the head
for this.
I will ask my artists
for the bits they don't use."

"Thank you, Madan Sara!
I'll bring you
something I carved
next time we come."
Inside, I'm leaping
and clapping.

Celestina nearly yanks me away,
throws a goodbye
to Madan Sara
over her shoulder.

"Wait! I have to ask her—"

I unfold the drawing of Fifina
I always carry with me
in my satchel.

"Have you seen her?"

Madan Sara looks closely.

"Pretty girl," she says,
shaking her head.

Celestina pushes me along.

"What makes you think
you'll find her here?

"And don't get a big head
about all this.

"Everyone thinks
they can sell what they make."

Celestina's words
do not discourage me.

My knife will find
the shapes in the wood.

Madame Williams

Madame's friends
from La Ligue Féminine,
the Women's League,
are here tonight.

They come every month
to talk about education for girls,

creating a safe place
where they can learn and live,
paying women for their work
instead of letting husbands and fathers
 control their money.

I wonder if all their talk
will make Madame Ovide
stop sending my pay
to Papa.

They even mention women voting.
I heard their first magazine
was closed down
for being just a little too critical
of the government.

But since their husbands
are all gwo zouzoun, gran nèg,
these white-gloved women
are allowed to keep meeting.

I like to listen in.

Maybe this
will be my way
back to school.

Madame Williams passes around photos
of her wood sculptures,
of girls who look like me

even though she is like the others,
rich and light,
and born in the city.

Madame Williams
says she will start
a free art school.

"Our nation's native genius
deserves to be unleashed."

                "Can I come to your school?"
                I hear myself ask.

The ladies fall silent,
eyes glued to their teacups.

Madame Ovide gives me a look:

Why can't you stay in your place?

"Everyone can come when
I open the school.
We'll build our own
center for art."
Madame Williams smiles
when she looks in my eyes.

I can't help beaming,
even when Madame Ovide
can hardly hide her scowl
as I clear the table.

"What good is art
when stomachs are empty?"
Madame Perez asks.

She ran the magazine
the government banned,
but is still the editor
of *La Voix des Femmes*.

Madame Williams
looks thoughtful.

"Our people's creations
inspired Picasso.

"They didn't believe
we had to choose
between feeding the body
and feeding the soul."

Invitation

Since our deal
at the market,
Celestina is nicer.

She's still angry
about the piano,
           but at least
           she decided
           I can do some cleaning
           inside again.
           Mainly I want to see
           Oreste's books,
           which I've only seen
           from his open door.

Celestina always cleans
his room,
but one afternoon
when she's away with Madame,
I sneak in.

His silver-framed photo
welcomes me.

"Petit Prince, why do you
look so sad? You have
the whole world
at your feet."

Madame said he'll be home soon.

I lie back on
his canopy bed
carved from mahogany
fit for royalty.

Then I go to his desk.
There's another framed photo,
of his father
sitting next to a man with darker skin
and a lion's mane
of bushy white hair.
Doesn't look Haitian. Maybe an Ameriken,
but not the kind
I saw in the Occupation.

The photo is signed
With all my esteem,
Frederick Douglass.

A magnifying glass,
school medals and ribbons,
a notebook filled
with coins and stamps
(some with his father
on them),

and an empty cologne bottle
with a label marked 1903.

Celestina told me
it had been specially mixed
in Paris
for his father
before he died.

I open it
to sniff
the few drops left
at the bottom.

Leather, tobacco,
sage, eucalyptus,
perhaps even
some pine

like my forest
back home.

His Books

have pretty
gold-lettered spines
and firm linen pages
that curl at the corners,
not cracked and moldy
like Sister Gilberte's.

They're filled with drawings
of plants, flowers, trees,
animals,

and are written by men
with strange-looking names:
Hugo, Rimbaud, Baudelaire, Mallarmé.

I choose one

Les Fleurs du Mal

and sneak open its pages,
inhale the scent
of wood pulp and ink.

At the top of the page,
"L'Invitation au Voyage."

Black-river words
crossing dry land.

Like the smell of chalk
          the smell of learning.

I want more

          without sneaking in
          and being afraid
          of getting caught.

JUNE 6, 1935

The Prince Returns

Madame Ovide
is so excited
her bracelets
can't stop dancing.

"He arrived late last night.
Paul drove him
from the harbor. Celestina
made him a honey-butter sandwich,
his favorite snack.

"Don't make a sound
this morning.
My dear son needs
his rest."

Madame has already boasted
about all his first prizes
in so many subjects,

the beautiful speech
he gave at his graduation.

Madame has already told me
about his bright future
after he studies
at Columbia University,
in New York.
After all we went through
with the Occupation,
I can't imagine why
her son wants to study
in America,
but I remind myself
that it's not my place
to ask questions.

"I knew my Ti Charlo was special
the day he was born

with a caul on his head,
like a king with his crown."

I don't know if he's really
all that special. Isn't every boy
considered more special
than a girl?

But Papa never made
me feel I was less special
than anyone else.
"Tout moun se moun"
is his favorite proverb.

What I do know
is Oreste has been
treated like a prince
entitled to his kingdom.

Yet I'm the one
who knows his every book,
every object
in his room.

And I have to admit,
I've dreamed
of him reading poems
to me
while I'm carving
for Madan Sara,
sitting on his bed.

Now that it's time
to meet him,
I'm afraid my dream

will be nothing more
than a gray-cloud field
of dry twigs and ashes.

Dous Lèt

This morning, I'm making
dous lèt.

Standing in the courtyard,
arms and shoulders aching
from stirring milk and sugar
with a wooden spoon,
I dab at my face
with my apron.

A few drops of sweat
fall into the pot.

> A pinch of salt
> makes it taste better,
> Cousin Phebus taught me.

The charcoal fire is
not too hot, just right.

Watch for warm milk bubbles
to rise to the surface,
circle the edges,
and thicken to caramel.

"Se anfans mwen."

He speaks in Kreyol,
his voice almost cracking.
"Smells wonderful.

Reminds me
of when I was a boy."

Without turning around,
I know it's him. I expected
a different kind of voice.
Commanding,
not cracked.

"Mèsi anpil, Mesye Oreste."
I clap my hand
over my mouth.

Will he tell on me?

"Don't worry about
my mother's 'No Kreyol' rule
with me. It hasn't worked so far.
And please call me Oreste.
'Mesye' was for my father."

           I like that he likes
           breaking that rule.

First Look

When I turn around to face him,
I try to smother
the surprise in my eyes.

He glows,
more beautiful than his photo.

Behind his glasses,
his eyes are a deep blue-green,

like the waterfall
near my village.

His eyes are shy,
but somehow
still make me feel
completely seen

in a way
I never expected.

Clear Water

"How do you know
when the dous lèt
is ready?" Oreste asks.

I tighten my grip
on the glass of water
to stop my hand
from shaking.
I drop a spoon of dous lèt
into it.

Trying to keep my mind
on his questions.

"You see?"
showing him the glass.

"When it's ready,
the water is clear,
not cloudy.

"The slower you go,
the better."

"Hmmm," he says,
looking at the glass.
My face
is growing hotter.

He looks away quickly.
"I think that's true
of most things in life,
but not all."

Does he mean
what I think he might mean?
Or something else?

The Line

"Like revolutions,"
he says, sitting on my stool
to watch me
take the pot from the fire,
pour out the dous lèt
onto the wood cutting board,
and spread it to dry.

Oh. A dip
of disappointment.

"What's your name?"

"Lucille."

Butterfly wings   beat hard against my ribs.

"Where are you from, Lucille?"

"I'm from L'Artibonite, Mesye Oreste.
From a village near Hinche."

"Just Oreste, please.
I can't be much older than you!"

"I'm sixteen."

"I'm just a year older. See?"

His smile
goes straight to my heart
like a sunray
piercing the clouds.

"L'Artibonite is our breadbasket,
feeding our whole country. We
should be thanking
all of you."

It's the first time
someone has thanked me
for being from home.
No idea what to say,
I focus on the the dous lèt.

"You're far from home.
I'm sure your parents miss you."

"My mother died
when I was born."

*Why in God's name
did I tell him that?*

It's the first time
I've talked about Manman
since being sent away.

"I'm sorry."
His voice is a gentle sea breeze,
not like any boy's
I've ever heard before.

When I finish spreading the dous lèt
and turn to face him again,
I lean back on the table,
lightheaded, weak-kneed,
as if I might faint.

"Is your father
still with us?"
he asks.

"Yes. He has his own
woodwork shop
in our village."

"That's good to hear. My father died
when I was ten. We were living
in Europe then. One morning
I went off to school, and when I came home
he was gone.
I never had a chance
to say goodbye."

Neither did I. Who would have thought
we'd have anything in common?

"My mother told me
that I shouldn't cry.
I was
the man of the house now,
and I needed
to be strong."

How could she tell him
not to cry?

I want to reach out
and hold him tight.

Celestina calls me
from inside.

"I have to go,"
I say, not wanting
to budge from the spot.

"I understand. It was
good to meet you. I hope
we can find some time
to talk again."

"I do, too,"
I say,
moving slowly away.

I wonder

                        if we've already crossed a line.

French

We don't have a chance
to talk again
until a week later.

Celestina and Madame Ovide
are going with Madame Perez
to a friend's summer house in Kenscoff.
Cousin Phebus will be there,
but they want me to stay

at Madame Ovide's
to start preparing
a dinner party
for a special Ameriken.

Madame has left me
a long list of things to do.
I start with
polishing the silver.

As soon as Madame's car leaves,
Oreste comes right out to the courtyard
and takes a seat,
as if he's been waiting
to pick up
where we left off.

"My mother does loves her silver—
and her gold!" We laugh,
feeling free, the house
to ourselves.

"Did you go to school
back in your village?" he asks,
"Because your French is so good,
and I know that in our country
education is not
the right it should be."

Pride, then a pang of sadness.
Missing Fifina, Sister Gilberte,
and those now lost days
of chalk and books.

"Yes. I went to a mission school,
run by the Sisters."

"Did you like it?"

"I loved it."
I try not to let
my voice quiver.

"I hated my school."

"Why?"

"It's the so-called best
school in the country,
the Lycée Saint-Louis de Gonzague.
But the Brothers teaching us
refused to let us learn
our own language and history."

*Still, I'd give anything
to be back in school.*

I look up from the serving spoon
I've been polishing. Oreste's face
is a tangle of anger and sadness.

"No Kreyol, of course. That goes
without saying. As if Latin and Greek
would be more important to learn
than the language
of our own land. They know
most people here
don't speak French,
but they didn't care."

"Well, *I'm* happy I learned French."

Because without it,
I couldn't read all the books
in your room.

I'm on the verge of confessing

but instead

pause to survey
all the forks, knives, and spoons
I need to polish.

Madame's silver storage box
is made of cherrywood
and lined with drawers
of dark-blue velvet.
I can't help admiring the wood,
wishing I could carve it.

A sigh slips out.

"Of course it's good to know both.
But only five percent of us
learn French, and in school they don't use
Kreyol to teach us, or teach us the language.

"French is the language
of the people who enslaved us.
Language is another form
of occupation. It keeps us
chained to them and their history.

"The history books we used
were French history. They started with
our ancestors, the Gauls!"

His laugh is bitter. "Of course,
I know my French family tree,
from Lorraine to Canada
to Louisiana, then Saint-Domingue,
because free people of color
and the Church kept records
of our births, marriages,
property, and wills."

He has a point. I don't
have a birth certificate,
but the Sisters
did write down
the date of my birth
and Manman's death.

"They wrote down
what they wanted to remember.
Definitely not the history of the Africans
who went to war
for their freedom.
They wrote about them
as if they were household objects,
with numbers next to them,
their value as property.

"Which is all we were
to them.

"How are the French
still making us pay
for our freedom?
Our ancestors already paid
with their lives.

"Why are we paying *them*
when they were the ones
who used us as slaves
and stole the riches of our land
from under our feet?"

My eyes are on the silver,
but my mind is on his words.

Paper Boats

With Oreste,
time passes faster,
but at the same time,
it slows down.

Sometimes, it even feels
like time stops.

Strange how
the two of us,
in just a few hours,
have made our own
paper boat
we're filling with stories.

It floats us
away from the shore
we both know
into a sea
of sun-dappled water.

Outside

I've finished polishing the utensils.
Now for the soup and serving bowls,
the champagne buckets.

"All this is well and fine
about the French.
But what about sòlda Ameriken yo?
You were in Brussels as a boy.
What do you know about the Occupation?"

"A lot. My father went to school
with the Caco resistance leader
Charlemagne Péralte.
The same school, Saint-Louis.
My father supported his friend
in secret, since he was
an ambassador, and the
Ameriken would have
gotten rid of him if he said
what he truly thought of them.
That's what they did
to those
who opposed the Occupation."

The champagne buckets
have grapevine handles
that are hard to polish.

Never have I been
so happy to polish them.

"Your mother says
you're going to study

in New York City.
Why do you want to go there?"

Oreste gets up
and brings his stool
next to me.

"I'll tell you
if you let me help you,"
he says.

"Fine. You can put all the utensils
back in their places."
I hand him the cherrywood box
with a mischievous smile.

Did he think
I wouldn't take him up on his offer?

He smiles, pretends to buckle
under the weight
of that cherrywood box.

"There's already a group of us
Haitians in New York, studying
at Columbia. New York
is where Harlem is. It's
where a movement
of the New Negro started.
That's what I really
want to see."

"Then you'll come back?"

"Of course. This
is home. My mother wants me
to be president one day."

"She's told us that before."

He laughs. "Sorry. I know
she talks about me a lot.
Like I'm doing now!"

I grin, nodding slowly.

Madame may be dreaming
that her son will be president,
and soar even higher
than his father,
but to me,
he doesn't seem
like the politicians I've seen
in our village festivals,
full of themselves
and putting on airs.
He's talking with me
and helping me polish
the silver.

The way that he talks
makes my sun inside
rise.

Tasting Dous Lèt

When we finish polishing,
I offer him
some more dous lèt
I made. This time,
just for him.

I take out my knife
and cut a slice
from the corner.

"That's a beautiful knife."

"Thank you. My father gave it
to me for my sixteenth birthday."

I'm about to hand him
the slice of dous lèt

when he leans his face close,
opens his mouth,
and puts out his tongue.

I feed him
a piece

without saying a word,
beaming so hard
my cheeks hurt.

He closes his eyes. His tongue
roams the sweetness.

"Li bon!"

"I'm glad you like it,
because it's the only thing
Celestina has let me cook so far.
My aunt moved in
after my mother died,
but I didn't learn this
from her."

"Then who taught you?"

"My cousin Phebus."

"She taught you well.
It has a special taste.
My mother mentioned
her. I was away at school then,
so we never met."

"I only see her once a month,
after Sunday Mass."

"May I please have some more?"
I like to hear him ask
for something only I can give.

"You've been a help to me,
so you deserve a reward."

I feed him another slice.

I know exactly
how delicious it tastes.

Another sweet secret
wrapping us closer.

A Warning

Celestina comes out
to the courtyard.
We hadn't heard them arrive.

"How is my Bébelle today?"
Oreste asks before kissing
her on the cheek.

"M'ap kenbe, Ti Charlo,"
she says with a smile
that turns into a frown
when she glances at me.

"Isn't it time
you set the table for dinner?"
I go inside quickly.
The hours crawl like crabs
when we're not together.

That night, as usual,
I keep my eyes lowered
when I serve Oreste dinner

even when he smiles
and thanks me by name.

Celestina notices.

"Don't think
I don't see
how you look
at him.

"Don't make this mistake.

"You're smarter than this.

"Do you want to lose
everything you've worked for?

"He will never be yours."

I don't care what she says.

The moments we steal
are a treasure I guard.

Sunday in July

Sunday after Mass,
I can't wait to see Cousin Phebus.
I want to tell her all about Oreste.
It's already July,
with the kind of weather you wear,
that weighs us down as we walk.

"Hello, Ti Cousine!
What's going on? Do you like it
at Madame Ovide's?
You look so much happier
than last month when I saw you,"
she says, tilting her head.

"I brought this from your father."
She hands me his package,
wrapped as usual in burlap.

This time it's birch,
so soft for carving.

My father's gifts
make me miss him more.

Like Fifina's gift.

In my dreams
I flip pages in vain,
desperate to find the recipe
that will bring her back.

"So what's making you smile,
like the world's at your feet?"
she asks.

"I met someone."

"Let me guess.
Is it a boy?"

I nod.

"I must say I'm surprised.
You were never the type
to fall for their nonsense."

"He's different
from any boy I know."

"Sure, he is.
Is he someone I know?"

I lean close to whisper.
"It's Oreste."

My cousin's mouth
makes a frozen O of surprise.

"Please don't tell me
you've fallen for him."

"I didn't say that. But every time
I see him, the sun rises inside me.
You know what I mean?"

She puts her arm around me
and sits me down on the park bench.

"My dear little cousin. You don't have a clue.
You know what he wants?

"Haven't you heard
all those stories

149

of light-skinned boys
from good families
who make it a game
to seduce servants like us?
Then we're thrown out
on the street
when we become pregnant.
We're just toys to them!"

"Why do you say that?
You don't even know him!"

"I know all I need to know.
But he's one of them,
not one of us.
It's as simple as that."

Her words hurt.
Does she think I'd be stupid enough
to be fooled
by those kind of seducers?

"I don't need to know him to know.
All men are alike.
If they can't sweet-talk you,
they'll find other ways
to get what they want."

"Oreste is not like that."

"Of course he is.
Men want one thing."

"Why do you say that?"

She squeezes my hand.

One Night

"I have to tell you a story
that you can never tell
anyone else. Promise?"
She's whispering,
so I move closer.

"Promise."

"There was an Ameriken. He'd been here
since the beginning. A marine, in charge of things
near us. A big man. Important.
He came to dinner once
as a guest of Madame Ovide."

*Hard to imagine Madame Ovide
inviting the invaders to dinner.*

"I know what you're thinking. But
when Madame Ovide returned from Belgium
a widow, she had to deal with the Ameriken,
or she would have lost all the property
the ambassador left her."

That explains it.

"Anyway, I was fifteen at the time. Already
helping in the kitchen, but that night I was also serving.
That man couldn't keep his eyes off me.
Madame Ovide pretended not to notice.
Maybe she didn't have much choice.
When he said he was going to the bathroom,
he came into the pantry instead,
where I was alone.

He closed the door behind him
and said we had to talk.
He said I should come live with him.
He needed a girl like me, to cook for him.
And take care of him
in other ways.
Then he tried to kiss me,
grinding himself into me.
When he wouldn't let go, I slapped him.
He looked completely shocked.
Called me a dirty Haitian whore
and said I'd be sorry."

Her hands grow clammy.

"He kept his word."

Her voice is flat and dry
but I feel her body tremble
just as it did
when she took me to Madame Ovide's.

"It was just a week later.
I was walking home from the market.
Suddenly his jeep was beside me.
There were
four of them. They grabbed me and threw me down
on the floor of the jeep, covered my mouth,
and brought me out to a field
far from the road.

"I begged him to leave me alone,
said I was just a girl.
'Wrong. You're just a whore,' he said.
He slapped me. Again and again.

Pinned me down. Told his friends
they should all take a turn
when he was through with me.

"They smelled like cigars.
When I tried to scream, he
burned my hand with one.
That shut me up."

I feel that island of flesh on her palm.
Her searing pain in the dry-twig voice.

"I passed out from the pain.
I don't how long it lasted, but it was dark
when they finally left me there.
I thought I might die there,
alone in the dark.
A farmer found me. Laid me across
the back of his mule,
carried me back to Madame Ovide's.

"She took me to the hospital.
She knew the director.
I stayed there for a week.

"The doctors and nurses took care of me,
as best as they could.
But they said
I could never have children."

When the tears stream down my cheeks,
I don't wipe them away.

I kiss the scar on her palm.
She sighs, makes a long exhale,
and turns away from me.

"Little Cousin,
promise
you will *never* tell anyone.
They will look at me different.
Like I'm dirty
and ruined."

"I promise.
I'm sorry. I wish—"

"No. No more wishing and dreaming.
Face the real world."

She stands up and drops my hand.
We walk on in silence.

An Offer of Help

The nightmare woke me,
and going back to sleep was impossible.
Cousin Phebus. So much pain.
I couldn't help my own cousin, but
the horror she lived through,
and the shame she still carries,
convinces me
that I must do absolutely everything possible
to find my friend.

I'll ask Oreste for help.

When he comes by that afternoon,
I show him my drawing.

"This is Fifina.
She was in school with me
before she disappeared.

"I think she was taken
by the section chief
to be his outside wife.
I also think he had her father
transferred to another prison
so she'd be completely
in his power."

The first time
I've told anyone
the whole story
I've pieced together
from the scraps of my nightmares.

I want to throw up.

Oreste takes the drawing
and studies it carefully.
His face fills with pain,
then a dark wave of anger.

"This is what happens
when the powerful
think they can do
whatever they want.

"Who needs the French
or the Ameriken to hurt us
when we do things like this
to ourselves?

"I'm sorry about your friend.
I'll help you find her."

In his eyes I now see
the young boy
who cried inside for his father.

Side by side we stand,
almost touching,
my drawing between us.

"How can you do that?"

I try very hard
not to sound too excited.
Oreste is the first person
who has offered to help me.

"My father had a very good friend,
the biggest publisher in Haiti.

"I can ask him
to use his mimeograph
to make copies of your drawing,
and I'll bring them to you."

Seven Copies

Two days later,
when he brings me seven copies
of my drawing of Fifina,
I hug him so tight that I nearly crinkle
them. Their ink smells like castor oil.

Seven copies.

"Thank you! I will leave some
 with Madan Sara
 at the Iron Market."

"Who is she?"

"She sells the wood polish I make
 and will sell my wood carvings
 as well.
 I'm saving
 to go back to school."

"Carving, too? On top
 of all your work?
 Do you ever sleep?"

Faraway questions.

I'm floating on the hope
 of finding Fifina.

"Will you show me
 your carvings?"

I almost never giggle,
 but today there's a reason.

"Only if you play the piano for me."

"Deal." We shake hands, but
 this time, he pulls me in close.

I close my eyes.

Wrap my arms
 around him,
 bury my face

in his neck,
as I did with Fifina.

He smells of fresh linen
and his father's cologne.

We hold each other
                              breathe as one

before I step back.

Celestina might show up
any second.

Might threaten
to tell Madame everything.

Or have me sent away.

                    You could lose everything.

He strokes my cheek
with his featherlight fingers.

The silence between us
wraps us soft as a blanket.

The Cross

It's already mid-July.
Oreste comes out to the courtyard
in the afternoons,
when he knows his mother
will be out
at her women's meetings.
But even then, it's rare
we can talk.

Ever since he gave me
the copies of my drawing of Fifina,
I have shown them
to everyone whose path I cross.

I feel close to him,
without needing to see him,
or even say a word.

When I'm alone,
and Celestina isn't nearby,
we talk a few minutes.
But there's rarely time
for more than just that.

Each time he visits
is like dous lèt in my day.

Except that one day,
when he showed me that photo.

"This is my father's friend,
Charlemagne Péralte.
He led the Cacos,
fighting the world's most powerful army
with its cannons and machine guns,
like David against Goliath.

"When they finally caught him

"they shot him in the heart

"threw his corpse on a mule

"lashed him to a door

"for everyone to see.

"Then they took pictures
and made sure we all saw them
to scare us from fighting.

"Instead, they created a martyr,
a hero we'll never forget.

"Yon Caco."

I stare at the photo,
sick to my stomach.

A glowing man
stripped nearly naked,
his pants at his feet
tied up on a door
like Christ on the cross.

Without thinking,
I make the sign of the cross.

Unroped

The men and the boys
roped together on the road
who I saw
when I was little,

this man in the photo
was fighting to free them.

"Péralte, along with
Toussaint Louverture,
our revolution's father,
are my heroes."

Oreste is a dreamer
in his own way, like me.

He says he is happy
the Occupation is over,
but there is still something
he can learn in New York.

"The Ameriken controlled our treasury,
our army, our police, and our courts.
Everything!"

And raped our women,
I want to add, but then remember
my promise to my cousin.

"I want to learn
how we can run our country ourselves,
without corrupt leaders
like Vincent and Trujillo."

When he talks like that,
I grow afraid
he might somehow end up
like the heroes he worships.

But I also
believe he is right.

When he talks about history,
he breathes it to life.

Maybe he's the reason
Madame holds her salons
with the white-gloved ladies
who will build schools for girls.

"All men and all women
should be equal in rights,"
he says. "Partners in life,
not divided by fear."

No wishes or dreams,
Cousin Phebus told me.

Yet I do wish
and dream

of a different world,
not divided by fear.

Carving Ice

Celestina says
Madame gave her money
to pay some artist in town
for an ice sculpture,
a centerpiece on the table
for her special dinner party.

"Why don't you do it instead
and we'll split the money?"
she whispers.

"But I have never even
seen ice before."

"Don't worry. I'm sure
it's not hard to do,"
she reassures me,
but doesn't offer

to lend me her icebox key
to let me have a look.

Since her warning,
she's always watching me.

I don't believe
carving ice will be easy.

What if Celestina is offering this,
hoping I will fail
and lose face
in front of Oreste,
Madame, and everyone else?

I already know
ice will be different
from wood.
No grain or rings.

Ice will rush me,
like a spring mountain
stream.

I find an art book
in Oreste's room
and choose a painting
to chisel in ice.

Hurricane Season

August,
hot and humid.
The time for
hurricanes,
like the one in my heart.

He'll be leaving
by the end of the month.

We don't find it easy
to steal time alone,
with Celestina
on the lookout.

I have to wake up
an hour early
so I have time
to carve for Madan Sara.

I brought her my first ones
last week,
and she thinks they will sell fast.
People will buy them
and also my polish.

I work on carving the
Madonna and Child.
All slightly different:
the grain of the wood,
the color and season.

Thank goodness Madame
is so busy with plans for
her big dinner party.

She spends afternoons
with Jeanne Perez
and the women of La Ligue,
whose promise of schooling
holds my future
in their white-gloved hands.

Our Inside Names

August is melting
like dous lèt on my tongue.

Oreste loves everything
that grows from the ground.

He sits for hours
in the garden and paints.

Sometimes he lies
down in the dirt
to get a closer look
at one little plant.

He doesn't seem to care
that his white shirts get dirty.
Celestina always
has a clean one ready.

One morning when I've finished
my work for the day

and Celestina is gone,
I bend near him to ask
what exactly he's looking at.

"That plant," he says.

He rolls over on his side,
his bright white shirt
stained with red earth,
and points.

A pair of thin leaves
joined at the heart
by a bright yellow fruit,
small hairy capsules
with three red-brown seeds.

The thin little plant
sags under its weight.

I stand up, back away,
brush the dirt from my knees.

"That's a weed,"
I say,
but there's something else.

Oreste rubs his hand
on his seersucker pants.

"A weed is a plant
whose virtue is unknown.
Do you know its name?"

I know the names
Fifina uses for plants,
but I don't think
they are the same in the city.

"In Latin it's called
Euphorbia pilulifera,"
says Oreste.

"Known by us here
as the asthma weed."

Then I remember.

"It's called hurts-your-hands
where I come from."

Oreste looks up at me,
almost ready to laugh,
but becomes serious again.

"Well, that's the first time
I've ever heard that.
But that's as good
a name as any.

"Things can have
many names, right?

"Like people.
I'm Oreste Charlemagne,

"or Ti Charlo
for short."

I smile at the nickname
I've heard Celestina use.
It's only for family,
and never outside.

Madame must have dreamed
of an emperor-king as her son.

"Do you have a nickname?"

            The one Fifina gave me.

"Ti Sè."

"That's nice,
but not for me to use with you.
What about Ti Zwazo,
like the little bird
in a song I love?

"It does make me think
of you."

My cheeks grow warm.

"Then it's perfect,"
I whisper.

Saying our inside names
wraps us even closer.

Serpent's Herb

I want to tell him
all about Mapou.

"With a tree,
you can climb it

"and hold it
in your arms

"and hear it sing."

He stands up
to face me,
red earth
on his clothes.

Does he think I'm crazy?

"I like what you say
 about the trees singing.

"Why wouldn't they?"

A breath of happy relief.

Like Fifina, he understands.

"Weeds are like trees
 that sing in small voices.

"I wish I could paint them
 and put them on stamps.

"I wish I could write
 a book about all of our plants

"with their names
 in Latin, French, and Kreyol.
 Then they could be studied
 in schools run by us."

"Great! Fifina and I
 want to start our own school.
 We want to write a book, too.
 You could come teach with us."

"That's a deal,"
 he says, shaking my hand.

I don't mind the red earth
 on my palm and my fingers.

I pluck up a handful
 to dry,
 just in case I need some
 one day,

for a recipe
from Fifina's book.

Now I remember
what else Fifina once said.

That weed's other name
is the serpent's herb.

AUGUST 15, 1936

Anniversary

Papa's piece of mahogany
arrived just in time
for me to start the carving
I will give Oreste
before his departure.

Cousin Phebus handed it to me
with a kiss but didn't talk again
about the horror
she lived through
that night.

Today, it's been two years
since the sòlda Ameriken
left.

And it's the Feast of the Assumption.

And our revolution
began in August.

So much to celebrate
all in one day.

And Madame's dinner party
is in three days.

And sooner than I want,
Oreste will be gone.

The Ice in August

He comes out to see me
after eating his breakfast,
right after Celestina
and his mother leave
for another trip to the market
before the Dinner Party.

I feel almost giddy,
because we know
we have time.

"I wish that one day
I could go to
Paris,"
I say.

"You might not like it.
It can be cold and gray,
and sometimes it snows."

I'd heard of cold winters
from Sister Gilberte,
and even saw her postcard
of snow
in the Ardennes.

I have a question
that I know could sound stupid,
but I ask it anyway.

Because I want to know.

"Is snow made of ice?"

"Snowflakes are crystals of ice."

Should I tell him?

"I'm carving the ice sculpture
for your mother's big party."

"What? She said
she was paying
an artist to do it."

He doesn't sound angry.
His lips curl in a smile.

"Celestina arranged it,
and we split the money.

"I need that money
to go back to school
one day,
then open a school with Fifina,"
I say, hoping he doesn't think
I always lie like this.

"You don't need
to explain. She's got more money
than all of us
could spend in our lifetime."

"Thank you. Now I don't
have to feel
as guilty."
We laugh.

"This may sound
a bit strange to you,
but I wish I could
really just
taste
some ice.

"Celestina may decide
she needs to watch
while I'm carving,
and of course,
I won't have much time!"

"Let's go, Ti Zwazo!

"It's a special day.
Off with your apron!"

Oreste takes my hand,
the first time
we're leaving
Madame's house together.

Celestina's warning becomes
melting ice in the sun.

Tasting Ice

At the street corner,
a graying man pushes his cart
lined with bottles of color.

"Bonjou, Machann Fresco,"
Oreste calls out.

"Bonjou, Mesye Ovide."

Machann Fresco eyes me,
his questions unsaid.

"We are celebrating
the day the sòlda Ameriken
left,"
Oreste announces.

The machann bows,
tips his cap.

He smiles
and picks up his scoop.

"What does your heart desire?
I have it all here.
Mango and guava
and fresh grenadine."

I point at the sparkling
ruby bottle of syrup.

"Grenadine it is.
What an excellent choice!"

He pulls back the burlap;
beneath it a block,
a crystal clear cube.

He shaves off some ice
from the top of the block
and uses a spoon
to shape a small dome.

"Wait," says Oreste.
"Lucille has never
tasted ice before."

Oreste turns to me
and takes both my hands.

"Let her taste ice
on its own first."

The machann places
a chunk of shaved pieces
in my palm.

I bring it to my lips
like the host at Communion.

"Ay!"

"What does it taste like?"

"I don't know. It's hard to say.
It tingles my mouth."

But I like it.

I see why Celestina
guards the icebox
with a key.

"Now the grenadine?"
asks the machann.
I nod my excitement.

With a delicate
flick of his wrist
the machann drizzles
grenadine on the ice
then hands it to me
in a white paper cone.

Oreste watches my face.

My palms are still tingling,
seared by the ice.

Mountains and Roots

After my feast of ice,
we walk back,
holding hands.

"Ti Zwazo, you do know
that our country is better
than anywhere else
because it's our home.

"We may not have snow
and ice on our mountains,
but our rain has passion
and our mountains
are magic.

"That's what Christopher Columbus
wrote when he and his pillagers
landed all those years ago."

Passionate rain
is one way to
describe the lavalas
and their deadly mudslides.

Oreste knows his history.

But I know our land.

Papa told me
our mountains
were once filled with fire
that carved rock
into caves
and made underground rivers.

I've seen times
when a brutal rain
battles
an even fiercer sun.

"The devil's beating his mother,"
Papa would say.

The devil smiles brightly
when his mother's tears flow.

I remember a day like that
when I would have been swept away
if I hadn't held tight
to Mapou's roots.

Aftertaste

When we get back to the house,
and he's leaving me in the courtyard,
Oreste stops.

"Thank you for that,"
he says.

"For what?"

"Celebrating with me.
Letting me watch you
taste ice for the first time."

We both laugh.

"I hope you enjoyed it
as much as I did,"
I say.

"I did."

We lean toward each other
and kiss. My lips still feel the tingle of ice,
now mixed with heat
that sends a ripple
through my body.

My first kiss on the lips.

I remember kissing
Fifina's neck. Her scent
of pine needles and sweat.

His of starched linen and eucalyptus.

Both so good

I know they'll return
in my dreams.

Trust Myself

When the block of ice is delivered
that afternoon,
I run outside to see it,
walk next to Paul,
who rolls it in a wheelbarrow
and sets it up
in the corner of the pantry

where my cousin first suffered.

Stomach turning, heart pounding,
I stare without moving.

Celestina stares at it, too,
no idea what I'm thinking.

"You've got no more
than six hours.
We will serve dinner
promptly at eight."

Thank goodness Celestina
urged Madame
to hire extra help.

A big smooth cube
of possibility,
like a summer morning.

I circle it slowly,
peer at it closely,
then close my eyes.

Papa would tell me
to look hard and listen
before I use my knife.

Of course with ice,
I'll be using an ice pick
and a chisel, but so far,
the ice isn't speaking to me,
unlike wood,
which always has something to say.

I try and see the shapes inside,
but at first I only see
bubbles of air and
unforgiving frozen water,
waiting to melt, a ticking time bomb
that melts instead of exploding.

Maybe this was not
a great idea.

The ice pick
feels clumsy in my hands,
and chunks of ice
splinter on the table.

I think of Papa.
He's taught me
I can trust myself
to know what's well done.

Coming in and out of the pantry,
Celestina says nothing.
Hard not to think
I may fail at this.

I take a deep breath,
slow down, use my own knife,
and trust myself
to shape Venus,
rising from a half shell
in the foamy sea.

I will spoon black caviar
at her feet.

I will give Venus
Madame Ovide's face.

Will she see
that I was the one
who made this?

The Dinner Party

Standing by French doors
in a new black uniform—
made to fit me—
the scratchy wool
digs into my skin.

The black patent-leather shoes,
also new,
are stiff and shiny
and hurt my feet.

Madame spared no expense.

My ice sculpture
sends waves of cool air
like a goddess wafting perfume.

Madame Ovide, the queen,
raises her glass for a toast.

"To all our guests,
especially Miss Katherine Dunham,
welcome to my humble home
in the Pearl of the Antilles.

"And to my dear son, Oreste,
who is leaving us too soon,
I wish a bon voyage."

In the soft glow
of candles
and the crystal chandelier,
she sparkles, a jewel.

Her gold-green eyes
meet the gaze
of each guest
one by one
before extending her arm
to Oreste.

He bows to his mother,
then turns and raises his glass.
"Merci à toutes et à tous. My late father
would have been honored,
as we are, to welcome you."

I expected more
of a speech
until I realize
that the memory of his father
is making him heavy
with sadness.

But for Madame,
the mood is triumphant.

Roast pheasant and grapes,
champagne shipped from France,
white roses in vases,
mahogany, marble, silver,
all polished and gleaming.

All our days of hard work
for one night of their feasting.

For me,
the evening's star
is the ice sculpture
I carved.

When the guests
enter the dining room,
they ooh and aah
at my creation.

Madame is like a cat
being stroked.
She soaks up the praise
before looking more closely.
"Yes, you're right. It *does*
look like me. The artist
certainly outdid himself!"

Celestina glares at me.

Is she unhappy
at the praise
she knows
is meant for me?

No guest is thinking
the ice sculpture
was made

by the girl
in the shadows,
clearing their plates
and refilling
their glasses.

The Athens of the Antilles

As I serve dinner,
I follow their talk.
They are all
speaking French.

What's new for Madame Ovide
is that men and women
at her table
are talking politics together.

Maybe Madame's white-gloved friends
are changing her. Everyone is going
around the table, introducing themselves
to the guest of honor,
yon fanm Ameriken
named Katherine Dunham,

who begins by thanking
her hostess and saying
she looks forward to
studying the rich folklore and dance
of Haiti.

This is a different kind of woman.
And Ameriken.

I overheard Madame say that
Mademoiselle Dunham
was not only well educated,
studying for the highest degree,
a doctorate, in something called anthropology,
but that she also was such an impressive
horse rider at the Jockey Club in Pétion-Ville,
that everyone was impressed.
Especially the men.

I couldn't stop staring.
She was petite and firm,
with the graceful movements
of a woman who knows
what her body looks like to others,
and likes how it feels to herself.

I could easily picture her on a stage,
in front of an audience,
hypnotizing them.

She looked happy in her skin
lit from within,
the color of oak,
just a shade darker than Madame.
When she smiled,

with her perfectly straight white teeth,
and spoke French
with a charming lilting accent,
the entire room was entranced.

Yes, this was the kind of woman
Madame wanted to stand
at her son's side
in the Presidential Palace.

My heart tightens
as I refill her glass.

Jeanne Perez,
whom Cousin Phebus went to work for
after that terrible night,
is the friend Madame
spends the most time with.

"Bonsoir à toutes et à tous.
We have read
so much about you,
Mademoiselle Dunham.
Please allow us to
introduce ourselves."

She turns to Madame.

"First, a toast
to our generous hostess,
a salonnière who cultivates
the finest minds of her nation,
as did Athena,
the goddess of knowledge."

Madame, blushing,
tilts her head slightly.

"You flatter me so!"
She places her hands,
with their blood-red nails,
on her heart.

"Not at all," Jeanne replies.

"Madame is the Athena
of the Antilles."

Madame is more like a cat,
arching her back for petting.

"My name is Jeanne Perez,
I'm editor of *La Voix des Femmes.*
I'm also starting
my own literary journal
and writing a play
on one of the Haitian Revolution's
greatest heroines,
Sanité Bélair."

Jeanne Perez, our own
Joan of Arc.

The woman next to her stands up.

"Mademoiselle Dunham,
my name is Suzanne Sylvain.
Like you, I'm an anthropologist,
completing my dissertation
on Haitian folktales
and our Kreyol language.

I'd be happy to help you
in any way I can."

Next to Suzanne
is her sister Yvonne,
studying to be a doctor,
a special kind
that helps women with their problems,
especially giving birth.

If she had been in my village,
perhaps she could have saved Manman
after I was born.
Not that the midwife
didn't do her best,
Papa told me.

Jeanne Perez and some others,
Madame Ovide told me, started
La Ligue
and its magazine, *La Voix des Femmes*,
the one Cousin Phebus reads.

Then their brother Normil
introduces himself as a poet,
and founder of *La Revue Indigène*,
"a journal dedicated to our culture."

I've seen Oreste with a copy.

The youngest brother, Pierre, is a botanist,
studying our trees and plants.
He and Oreste have been
in deep conversation
since his arrival.

Pierre stands to toast the ancestors:

"To our father, Georges,
whom we lost eleven years ago,
God rest his soul.
A celebrated poet, lawyer, and diplomat,
a good friend to Ambassador Ovide,
who also took a principled stand
against the Occupation.

"To our uncle Benito,
who organized a Pan-African Conference
in London, back in 1900,
where he represented both Haiti
and Ethiopia. He was
an aide-de-camp to Emperor Menelik II,
who led the Ethiopian people
in driving out the Italians.

"All those years ago,
our uncle Benito
believed Haiti and Africa
should have closer ties
to fight the whites
ruling their countries,
to fight colonialism,
which they saw
as a new form of slavery.
May their fight for justice
continue to inspire our own."

Pierre sits down
to applause from the guests.

Oreste looks enthralled.

It's clear he admires both Benito
and Georges Sylvain,
heroes in the struggle
he himself wants to fight.

Only then
does it hit me.

I am in the midst of
people who care
about our history
and culture.
People I'd heard
being made fun of
at the market
for being absent-minded
professors,
their heads in the clouds,
or white-gloved ladies,
teacups in hand.

People some say have
never known
an honest day's work.

Yet here they are.

They want us
to know our own history,
to chart our own future,
to connect the past
to the present.

No wonder the French
and the Ameriken

were still making us pay
for daring
to believe we deserved
to be free.

Yes. I see it now.

I know it is
exactly someone like Jeanne Perez,
or someone from une grande famille
like the Sylvains,
the kind that makes history,
that Madame would like
her Charlo to marry into.

He catches my eye
and smiles,
and despite my own sadness,
I smile back.

Politics

I go in and out of the kitchen,
refilling glasses
and bringing new plates
of Madame's
gold-trimmed porcelain.

My stomach is growling.
I had no time
to eat
between carving the ice
and preparing this dinner.

Now I'm lightheaded,
trying hard to steady my feet.

In the kitchen,
when no one is looking,
I gnaw on the bones
of the pheasant,
scoop up
wild rice and asparagus
from the plates.

Back in the dining room,
I catch a few more names
and more words.

Jean Price-Mars
is also an anthropologist
and writer. It's clear
from their faces at attention
that all the guests respect him.

Yet his skin is almost
as dark as mine.
Not all the important people
in our country
look white,
thank goodness.
There's hope.

"Professor, I've read your fascinating book
on Haitian customs and folkways,"
says Mademoiselle Dunham
to Professor Price-Mars.

"Do Haitians feel ready
to govern themselves,

now that the Occupation is over?"
she asks.

"The Occupation helped us unite
against a common enemy," says
Jeanne Perez.
"Excuse me, Professor, for jumping in."
The professor nods with a smile.

"But we do know
that democracy is
as fragile as an orchid,
which can wither
in the wrong soil.

"Look at Hitler,
helping Mussolini invade Ethiopia,
helping Franco
bomb his opponents. Never mind
what he's doing in his own land.

"I have it
from reliable sources,
my journalist friends,
including those who've escaped,
that Hitler sends those who oppose him
to a hellish prison called Dachau,
and just a handful
have lived to describe it.

"Weren't their nations
once democracies?

"If Europe cannot
defend herself
from vile men

who crave power,
then who are they
to lecture us?"

Mademoiselle Dunham nods
but asks,
"Europe has been a mess
since the Great War,
but is there a tradition
of democracy here?"

"With respect,
is there one in America?"
replies Jeanne.

"From what we see,
democracy doesn't extend
to all our people. Your great
Professor Du Bois,
whose father was Haitian,
has written about
the American Negro's
'double consciousness.'

"It's clear to us, especially after
the Occupation,
that American democracy
has a double standard."

I nearly drop the stack of plates
I'm balancing on my way to the kitchen,
from both hunger and shock.

It's the first time I've heard
a woman talk about politics,
especially like that.

In my village, that kind of talk
was always left to the men.

Bravo, Jeanne!
I want to jump up and shout.
If only I weren't
a hungry girl
in the shadows.

The Talk at the Table

Jeanne is sitting next to
a thin light-skinned man,
whose name I missed.
His gold-rimmed pince-nez
sits high on his nose.

"Are you saying
that all Americans
are imperialists?"

"Of course not,"
says Jeanne.
"Look at all the Negro
newspapers and leaders
who spoke out against
the Occupation.
But most Americans
don't even know
they are part
of an imperialist culture.

"Excuse me for saying this,
Mademoiselle Dunham,

since you are our honored guest
and we appreciate your serious study
of our culture,
but when it comes to history
and geography, Americans seem to be
willfully ignorant."

Mademoiselle Dunham simply smiles
and seems not to take offense.

Unlike Pince-Nez.

"The problem, Mademoiselle Perez,
is not American ignorance,
but our own.
It is precisely the customs
and folkways
that Mademoiselle Dunham
and others want to study.

"The common Haitian peasant
is not in any way
ready for democracy,
because he truly believes
in magical thinking."

He won't even say
the word vodou.

"We need science
and modern thinking
to govern ourselves.
The old ways
are holding us back.
That is why President Vincent
supports the laws against them.

How can we be
the Athens of the Antilles
if our people
believe in nonsense?"

Pince-Nez takes off his glasses
and rubs them clean
with his white linen handkerchief.

His question hangs in the air.

Jeanne Perez folds her arms.

Oreste speaks up.

"It isn't our traditional ways
that damage democracy,"
says Oreste. His mother
shoots him a look of warning,
but he continues.

"Look at how General Trujillo
runs the Dominican Republic.
Vodou isn't the problem.
The problem is
that he openly cavorts with people
who do terrible things
and stirs up trouble
at the border.

"He inflames his people
with speeches
against us.

"He says Haitians are weeds
that should be
pulled up,

black vermin infecting
his people's 'white' blood.

"Isn't that ironic,
when we all know
his own grandmother
was Haitian
and he uses bleach
and makeup
to lighten his skin?"

Nervous laughter escapes
from most of the guests
before Oreste continues.

"That sounds a lot to me
like how the National Socialists
in Germany
talk about people
who do not see things
their way.

"They clearly announce
the 'enemies of the state,'"
he says, then goes on,
counting on his fingers:

"The Jews, of course.
We've seen the photos
of the boycott
back in '33.
'Juden' painted on buildings,
on broken-glass storefronts,
shopkeepers trying
to sweep up the chaos.

The same year, they banned
political opponents,
the Social Democrats, the Communist Party,
and trade unions.

"I've heard from some friends
who used to frequent
Berlin's nightclubs
that severe new 'race' laws
will be passed
against Jews.

"But that's not enough.
There are Jehovah's Witnesses, even some Catholics,
gay men and women,
cross-dressers, jazz lovers,
'degenerate' artists, handicapped people,
anyone seen as 'unfit'
for the 'pure' Aryan nation.

"And the list goes on!

"I'm only reporting
what my school friends in Europe
are writing to me.
They live in Belgium,
where I was born,
where my late father
was ambassador.

"We at this table
all know German Haitians
who have been here
since right after independence.

In our own family tree
is a Jewish German.

"Hitler and his party
hate all of us, too.

"My friends just returned
from Berlin
for the Summer Olympics.
Everything was spotless,
with glorious pageantry.

"The trams and the trains,
all ran like clockwork.

"Yet Hitler was so furious
that a Negro athlete
won four gold medals
that he refused
to shake hands
with that victor,
Jesse Owens.

"Doesn't that tell you
what's beneath all the show?"

Oreste looks around the table
and puts up his hands.

"Please don't shoot.
I'm only the messenger!"

Laughter erupts, like pent-up relief,
from nearly every guest.

"But the situation is serious
here, too.

Trujillo is close
to some of those Germans.

"He is playing with fire.
His words fill people with hate,
the kind that leads people to kill.

"Why doesn't our own president
restrain his so-called friend,
especially at the border,
and stand up for us?"

Silence. No laughter
when it's so close to home.

Pince-Nez clenches his jaw
and stares coldly at Oreste.

Madame clears her throat
and shifts in her chair.

"Please excuse my son,"
she says to Pince-Nez.

"You know how
rash the young can be. Their fervor
overtakes their manners.
All of us here
greatly appreciate and are loyal
to our president,
as much as my late husband was."

Her words drip with honey,
then she changes the subject.

When I look at Oreste,
his face is unrepentant.

He turns slowly away
from his mother.

I am proud of him and Jeanne,
but fear gnaws at me, too.

Couldn't
what's happening there
happen here?

It's not as if
we haven't known
terror before.

He looks up at me,
then at my Venus,
and winks.

> *Our secrets are growing.*

From across the room,
Celestina is staring me down.

From the eyes of my Venus,
glistening tears melt.

What Paris Is Like

Two days later,
while his mother is visiting
Jeanne and her friends,
basking in the afterglow
of her triumphant dinner,
and Celestina is with family
in Jacmel,

Oreste comes to see me
in the courtyard.

No mention of
his defiance at dinner.

Perhaps his mother scolded him
in private.

"You said you wanted
to visit Paris. Surprise!"

He carries brightly painted postcards
from Paris, otherwise known,
he tells me, as the City of Lights.

"My father bought me these
on our first trip to Paris
to visit his good friend
Dantès Bellegarde, who was
the minister plenipotentiary.
My first memory is watching
the Bastille Day parade with them,
perched on my father's shoulders.

"I loved that even more
than when we visited Waterloo,
where Napoleon
was defeated."

He spreads out the postcards
like a deck of cards.
"Which do you want
to visit first?"

I choose one
at a time.

He tells me
the story behind each
of the cards.

Notre-Dame Cathedral,
majestic and proud
stands on Île de la Cité.

La tour Eiffel,
unloved and unwanted
at first,
now a symbol of Paris.

Le Louvre museum,
where he saw the world's
most famous painting,
the *Mona Lisa.*

He knows the history
of each place pictured.

He shows me
the Canal Saint-Martin,
with its green-iron bridge.
"That's the Place de la République,
named in honor of the French Revolution.
The French make sure their history
is in everyone's face."

That night I dream of us
floating on a flower-covered barge
on the Canal Saint-Martin.

It feels a lot sturdier
than our paper boat.

Drums

At the dinner party
Pince-Nez implied vodou
was holding Haiti back.

Some city people
even helped the blans
take away the temple drums.

But most people
in my village have statues
of the Catholic saints
next to shrines
for the lwa.

Drums in the night
could mean secret meetings
of vodou or fighters—
not exactly the things
those in power want.

Papa even helped
neighbors hide drums
in the forest
to keep them safe.

He didn't go to the temple,
but he never said
anything bad
about the gods.

Why not be
protected by both?

I need all the help
I can get.

I can no longer pretend
I'm not falling in love.

An Unsuitable Wife

Madame can talk all day
about improving
the condition of our women
and making sure all of us
can read and write

but she'd never let
her little prince
marry me.

I have no money,
no famous family,
and have dark skin to boot.

Celestina is right.

At best, Madame *might* accept me
after she marries him to
the right girl
from the right family,
like the Sylvains.

Only then
might Madame allow
her only son
an outside wife.

The one who must always
stay in the shadows,
like a mistake covered up.

An indulgence,
expected of the powerful man
her son is sure to be.

I can tell
he feels the way I do.

But since Oreste is leaving soon,
Madame Ovide and Celestina
want more of his time.

We know
we must be more careful.

Still, he sneaks out
to see me,
and it takes all our will
not to kiss again.

His voice is gentler than before,
though now his eyes burn brighter.

"Haiti is the Pearl
of the Antilles,"
says Oreste.

"The French say
our country reminds them
of their beautiful Riviera.
I think it's better."

"If you love it here so much,
why don't you stay?"

"There are things
I must do first.
But I'll come back.
I promise."

"You might forget me
when you go away."

"Do you truly think
that I can ever forget you?
Love is like water,
which never forgets
its home."

But will love
carve a cave in my heart
and fill it with
ash and tears?

Little Bird

Oreste will soon
board the ship to New York.

Since being sent away
from home,
I no longer dream every night,
but when I do,
I wake up even earlier
to keep it fresh in my mind.

Last night's dream
was of three red-bottomed birds
perched next to each other
in my happy Mapou.

So now I take
my knife to slowly shape
the glowing mahogany
Papa sent me.

My fingers
feel clumsy,
the knife slips away.

I can't carve this
as perfect as my dream.

Oreste is busy
saying goodbye to family,
to all his school friends.
A last trip to the tailor
for his shirts and his suits,
and then to the barber
for a proper haircut.

At last
when everyone
is out of the house
Oreste takes me inside
to the piano.

"I want to play this for you
before I leave.
I wrote down
the words for you—
they're from a poem
written in Kreyol."

"People write poems
in Kreyol?"

"Not many right now,
but more will learn.

"The song
is called 'Choucoune'
and the words are by Oswald Durand,
one of our greatest poets.

"It's about
the beauty
of our women here.

"But of course,
it's about you."

Ti Zwazo

"Ti zwazo nan bwa ki t' apé kouté
Ti zwazo nan bwa ki t' apé kouté
Kon mwen sonjé sa
Mwen genyen lapen
Ka dépi jou-sa
De pyé mwen nan chen
Kon mwen sonjé sa
Mwen genyen lapen
De pyé mwen nan chen."

>   *Little bird who listened deep in these woods*
>   *Little bird who listened deep in these woods*
>   *When I think of this*
>   *It brings me such pain*
>   *Ever since that day*
>   *Both my feet in chains*
>   *When I think of this*

It brings me such pain
Both my feet in chains.

His voice fades
to little more
than a whisper.

> When he finishes playing
> he takes the bird-step paper,
> rolls it up,
> ties it with a
> a ribbon,
> and hands it to me.

> "You are the best thing
> that's happened to me.
> Thank you."

> I hurry away
> so he won't see
> my tears
> of joy
> and sadness.

Wings

Later that night,
after all the lights are out,
we meet outside.

"I made this for you."

I unwrap my gift for him
slowly, with care.

Three little birds,
their heads touching,
perched on a branch
of Mapou.

Wood glowing from inside
with my olive wood polish.

He touches it in silence,
peers at it close.

"It's beautiful. Thank you.
I'll keep it with me
wherever I go.
Who is the third little bird?"

"Fifina."

"If anyone can find her,
it will be you," he says.

He stands the small carving
the size of my palm
next to him on the stone bench.

The sounds of the night—
crickets, frogs, dogs—
embrace us.

In the full-moon night
we see each other
even more clearly.

My carving watches over us
from the bench.

I take his right hand

lead him from the courtyard
to the garden

run my fingers
through his curls.
How long I've wanted
to do this. Why
did I wait?

My lips are drawn

to the hollow in his neck

a butterfly kiss.

> He pulls me up
>
> to the pillow
> of his mouth,
>
> for that long kiss
> we've both wanted
> since the first one.
>
> A long kiss that shakes me,
> burns through me,
> then flows down
> through my feet,
> like the roots
> of Mapou.

Greetings

"A letter!"
cries Madame Ovide,
gold bangles jangling.

"Please, Madame,
read it out loud,"
begs Celestina.

I try to look
completely absorbed
in the fish soup
I'm ladling.

"All right. He says, 'Harlem
is much better than Paris.
There's a movement
of *black people*
from all around the world
who believe we should be
united. They call themselves
Negroes.'"

Madame
reads his letter,
disbelief in each word.

"*Negroes*?
From *nègre*—and *nèg*?"
She sighs and shakes her head.

"My son is Haitian,
from une grande famille.
Has he completely forgotten

who he is
and where he's from?"

What's wrong with Negro?

Of course
everyone in Haiti
knows that a nèg
is a person,
plain and simple.

Tout nèg se nèg,
like tout moun se moun.

All people are people.

"He says, 'Columbia
is perfect
for studying the law.
I'm learning so much!

"'My English is improving
every single day.
And the people I meet!
We fight against lynching,
which happens not just
in the South here.
We fight for our rights
to be treated as equals.

"'Tout moun se moun!'

"Now he's *writing*
in Kreyol?"
groans Madame.

"'I'm meeting honorable men,
such as James Weldon Johnson,
who came to Haiti in 1920
and spent years exposing
the brutal truth of the Occupation.
He and the National Association
for the Advancement of Colored People
are true friends to our nation.

"'As is the magnificent poet
Langston Hughes,
who wrote *Popo and Fifina*
and published a letter last May
decrying the imprisonment
and demanding the release of—'"

Madame frowns,
squints at the letter.

"He crossed out his name.
Oreste knows
Jacques Roumain,
a sworn enemy
of our president,
is back here in jail.
And now he brings up
that infamous letter!
The last thing my son needs
is to spend time
with even *more* Communists!"

She fans herself
with the letter,
then turns the page.

"'In the mornings,
I go walking in Central Park,
which is near
my apartment in Harlem.
The birds there
are impressive,
but in no way
as glorious as ours,
nor will their song
ever be
as sweet to my ears.'"

She looks up to the heavens.

"My only son. May he grow wiser
in his time away.
Spend more time
studying and bird-watching
than indulging in dangerous politics.

"What a letter!
Oh, and he sends
his warmest greetings
to all of the servants."

Is Celestina checking my reaction,
or am I imagining things?

His Letter

Greetings. Servants.

Oreste's words are
the stings of a wasp

when the words
I want most

are impossible
for him to write
in a letter back home.

I try to squeeze
all the hope I can
from his only letter.

What he wrote about birds:
Could that have been
his secret message
to me, Ti Zwazo?
Why else mention birds
in a letter to his mother?

My heart is somersaulting
between doubt and faith.

I force myself to carve
but everything takes more effort
since our goodbye.

Celestina still keeps
her share of my coins.

I save my own coins,
stuffed in a sock
under my mattress.

After I cry,
I pray my three birds
will keep him safe
until he returns.

After

It feels like a lifetime
since the kiss,
that last night
in his arms.

And then that letter.

I have no way
of writing him back.

At first, I lit
a candle for him at Mass.

Then I stopped going.

What's the use?

I'm tired
of losing everyone
and everything
I love.

I whisper his name
in my prayers at night,
like I do Fifina's,
but Bondye
is too busy to listen.

Outside
I'm a shadow girl,
doing what I'm told.

Inside
I'm a bird,

beating her wings
against a cold cage.

I get even thinner
because nothing tastes good
in a cage.

My skin still tingles
when I remember
each touch
each kiss.

When we were together
we were a harbor
for each other,
our folded paper boat
our flowered raft,
safe in the storm.

How can I build
my own harbor inside
when all that I love
is taken away?

Betrayed

Celestina had Paul drive me
alone to the market today.

I ask Madan Sara
about Fifina.

"I'm sorry. I show this
to everyone I can.

With all the money you're making,
you could offer a reward," she says.

My heart tightens like a fist.
For the past month,
Celestina has given me
much less than before,
even though Phebus told me last Sunday
that Madan Sara was selling everything I make.

"Business is slow,"
said Celestina with a shrug.
"I told you not to expect too much."

Celestina was lying.
Now I see why.

"Madan Sara, how much would you say
I've sold this month?"

"At least twenty gourdes.
That's a lot for someone new—and so young.
You should be proud of yourself,"
she adds with a nod.

"Thank you, Madan Sara.
I will keep bringing you more.
From now on,
please set aside my money.
I will collect it myself."

When I reach Madame Ovide's house,
I'm breathing hard, and my fists are coiled tight.
In the kitchen, I tap Celestina on the shoulder.

"Where's the rest of my money?
I just saw Madan Sara . . ."

Celestina doesn't turn around.

"The rest of your money
is to keep my mouth shut."

"What?"

"I deserve to keep more.
I saw you with Oreste
that night in the garden. I warned you
so many times. And don't forget:
I'm the one who brought you
to meet Madan Sara.
You'd be nothing
without me.
And this is how you repay me?"

"But Oreste and I, we only—"

Celestina turns slowly to face me,
looks me up and down,
disgust and anger flaring her eyes.
"Who do you think you are?
You think
you're better than I am?"

I feel like grabbing her shoulders
and shaking her,
but I don't dare. She could easily
knock me to the ground.

"He doesn't *belong* to you,"
my voice trembles.
"We *love* each other.
You can't stop that."

"Oh, really?" she says,
   drying her hands on her apron.

"Watch me."

In Her Place

For the rest of the day,
I avoid Celestina.

After dinner,
she follows Madame
upstairs.

I wait a bit,
then sneak up to listen
outside Madame's door.

"At the market, Madan Sara
   told me an American lady is looking
   for a house to rent. She has
   money to pay you well,"
says Celestina. I hear her
brushing Madame's hair.

"Why don't you
   rent her one of your houses
   at an *American* price,
   and send Lucille to work there
   for the same price you pay her here?"

Celestina's revenge.

I never thought
she would go this far.

"I have a sweet cousin
who would be so happy
to take Lucille's place.
She works harder,
talks a lot less,
and she costs a lot less."

"Why do you want me
to send Lucille away?"
I hear Madame ask.

"Because she doesn't know
how to stay in her place.
She thinks she's better
than all of us servants.
People like that
don't stop
until they get what they want."

"And what exactly is it
that Lucille wants?"

"Your son."

Madame groans.
The hairbrush falls silent.

"Madame, I warned her
over and over to stay away from him.
But the night before he left,
I saw her
lure him into the garden.
God only knows
what happened there."

Madame sighs deeply.

"When Ti Charlo comes home
for Christmas," adds Celestina,
"I know that girl will start chasing him again.
What if she makes a baby for him?"

A sharp crack splits open
the cliff in my heart.

Dreaming of Him

You were in night water. I watched from the shore.

My Love, My Light.

The tide held you firm in her arms. The farther you went, the louder

I screamed. No sound from my throat.

Only sharp shards of ice.

The harder I screamed, the farther you floated.

I tried to make my voice a rope you could catch.

A rope to bring you back.

I tried to follow you into the water, but my whole body stiffened.

My torso became a tree trunk.

My arms sprouted leaves.

My legs sank deeper into soft red earth.

My toes grew long, like the roots of Mapou.

I tried to follow you into the water, but my body, a tree, would not

let me.

When you called my name one last time,

there was no fear in your voice

                       before the waves

                       drowned you in darkness.

Leaving

I will pretend not to know.

What else can I do?

Celestina avoids me.

A week later,
after I bring Madame her breakfast,
she tells me to stay.

"An American woman
is renting one of my houses
for several months."

I stare down at the rubber sandals
chaining my feet.

I've never even talked
to one of *them*.
And if I had any choice,
I never would.

Not after the Occupation,
not after what they did
to those poor souls in ropes,
to Charlemagne Péralte,
to our whole country.

But on the other hand,
Mademoiselle Dunham
was different. Perhaps it's her.

"What's her name?"

"Mademoiselle Hurston,"
says Madame.
"Just call her Mamzelle.

"Celestina's cousin
Joseph will be her driver.
He'll stay in the basement,
where his wife and baby can visit.
Joseph will pick you up
in an hour.
It's too far to walk."

That soon.

"You'll stay in the maid's room
next to Mamzelle. You're lucky
to be working for her.
Of course
your pay will go
to your father."

Lucky girl. Again.

"Now, go pack.
Everything else you need
will be at the house."

Celestina left early for the market
and she hasn't returned.
No wonder. Everything has already

been planned
to send me away.

"Americans have dollars,
but don't ever trust them.
Remember the past."

Cousin Phebus.
I bite my lip hard.

"But what about Mademoiselle Dunham?
She was your guest of honor . . ."

"She was different, a friend of our friends,"
she snaps back. "The exception proves the rule."

I've never understood that saying.

Madame is staring hard at me,
as if she wants me to know
that she knows about Oreste.
"Remember that
just because Mamzelle's skin
is the same color as ours
doesn't mean
you can trust her.

"I'm giving you
one last chance
only because your mother
and Fifina's
helped me
when I was your age."

"What happened?"
I blurt out,
surprising myself.

"None of your business. This time,
be *absolutely sure*
you stay in your place."

Our mothers helped her.
So who is she,
or Celestina,
or Tante Lila,
or anyone else,
to tell me my place?

PART THREE
LAWOUT

OCTOBER 1, 1936

Mamzelle

A dry goodbye from Madame.
She does not mention
exactly how long I will be gone.

Sitting in the back of this car,
I twist myself to see her house
until I can't anymore.

Joseph is silent. From time to time,
his mustache twitches.

We're heading away
from the city,
to another fancy neighborhood
up in the hills,
called Pétion-Ville.

Sharp turns snake the hills
like the road
from my village.

When I arrive
at the house Mamzelle is renting,
the front door is unlocked.

Joseph brings me through
a big sunlit parlor
to the kitchen.

No chandelier or gleaming piano.
No garden with fountains and flowers.

Still, a beautiful house
high in the hills with a view of the city
and serenaded by birdsong.

I could picture
Oreste and Fifina and me
happy here.

Joseph interrupts my daydream.

"As soon as you hear
she's awake,
bring her breakfast in bed.

"Strong black coffee
with red sugar.

"Cassava bread,
spread with peanut butter,
and sliced mango.

"I went to the market
this morning."
He points to the basket
on the kitchen counter
and leaves.

Joseph's voice
was as dry as Madame's.

Did I expect
anything different?

Preparing Mamzelle's breakfast,
I wonder: Why does she
wake up so late?

I hear a yawn from the bedroom.

I snatch at the breakfast tray.
The cup and the saucer
rattle like chains.

My face is a pinewood mask.
I knock loudly.

"Entrez!"
says a voice
in a lazy, strange accent.

Mamzelle is arching her back
and rubbing her neck.

I try to remember
Cousin Phebus's warning:

The tallest tree
is always chopped down first.

Rings Tell the Truth

I stand in the doorway
until Mamzelle motions me in.

From a distance
Mamzelle is no older
than Madame Ovide

but the rings on her neck
are deeper up close.

"Right here is fine,"
says Mamzelle in a French
I've never heard before.

She pats the bed with her hand.

"Oui, Mamzelle."

"You can call me Zora."

"Oui, Mamzelle Zora."

Even her name
sounds strange to my ears.

I put down the tray
and step away from the bed.

Mamzelle sips her coffee.

"Mmmm. C'est bon."

She dunks the kasav
into her coffee,
doesn't even look down
when it splashes on the saucer.

"Le déjeuner à midi, s'il vous plaît."

"Si'l *te* plaît," I blurt out
before remembering Madame's warning
to stay in my place.

I know she would say
it isn't my place
to correct Mamzelle's French.

Even if Mamzelle doesn't know
she shouldn't use *vous*
with a servant.

"Your French is very good,"
Mamzelle says, drinking her coffee.

"I can teach you English.
Would you like that?"

A small nod.
Though my mask remains steady,
my heart
twirls with joy.

"I'll be out a lot
for my fieldwork.
That means talking to everyday folks
and learning and seeing how they live."

To learn English
would give me wings,
like learning French.
Oreste is speaking English
in New York. I'll learn enough
to write him a letter in English,
and his mother
won't understand it
if she gets her hand on it.

Maybe I can even
find a way to get Mamzelle
to help me find Fifina and
go back to school
and start our own.
After all,
the Ameriken are rich.
They pay in dollars.

Or maybe
this will just lead   to more cliffs   and dreams
burned to ash.

"If Mamzelle Zora would like."

I try to make
my voice a little warmer
but without inviting
her any closer.

"Would Mamzelle
like anything else now?"

"Non, merci.
I'll be writing now.
Whenever this door is closed
or you see me reading or writing
anywhere at all,
don't disturb me.
That means I'm working."
I close the door.

I will leave lunch for Mamzelle
covered on the terrace
and dinner inside.

Since I know how
to do my chores quickly,
and she hasn't asked me
to do anything more,
working for her
might leave me more time to carve!

This may not be
as bad as I thought.

Rings That Can Vanish

Breakfast next morning
dashes my hopes
of being left to myself
and having time for myself.

"Are all your beds this small?"
asks Mamzelle.

"Looks like
they're meant
to be in a convent."

Mamzelle tilts back her head,
laughing loudly.

The lines on her neck
disappear.

I don't know
what to say.

"How old are you?"

"Sixteen."

"You look younger.
That will be good
when you're *my* age.
Are you married?"

I shake my head,
hoping she can't see
my eyelids twitching.

"No boyfriend?"

My lips tighten.

Will Mamzelle be
a woman
who always asks questions?

Another Life

On a desk by the window
is a stack of white paper,
some pencils, a red notebook
with loose pages peeking out,
a leather-bound scrapbook
like Sister Gilberte's,
something wrapped in brown paper,
and a shiny black typewriter,
even bigger
than the one at the police station.

That was the last time
I held a pencil.

Another life.

There was a crucifix
above the bed.

It's now on the bottom row
of the bookshelf.

Madame Ovide
would not be pleased.

I know she hasn't invited
Mamzelle to dinner,
as she did Mademoiselle Dunham.

Mamzelle is certainly
different.
Her nonstop smoking.
That desk, overflowing.
I can't help staring.

"You want to know
what all this is for?
I can tell you all about it
if you help me with my work."

"What work?"

"I need someone I can trust
who knows Kreyol inside out
for my studies on voodoo."

I remember that tourist,
and the dinner
and what Pince-Nez said.

"Why do you
want to study that?"

"Because it's important
to me, and it should be
to the world."

I back away.
"I can't help you with that.
Sorry."

Mamzelle is inviting
trouble to the table.

She shrugs off my no,
but I can tell
it won't be
the last time she asks.

The Dead

It's been a month,
and the shape of the days
is clear to me now.

Mamzelle was gone
the past two days
for the Fèt Gede,
the Feast of the Dead,
at the cemetery,
laughing, singing, drumming,
drinking kleren,
to raise the dead.

Not exactly how the Sisters
taught us to celebrate
the Day of the Dead
and the Day of All Souls.

So it's no surprise
when she wakes up around noon
with bloodshot eyes,
has lunch in bed,
then closes her door
to write.

Sometimes I hear
the quick clack-clack
of the typewriter;
other times I imagine
the soft scribbling of her pencil
in that red notebook.

When she comes out for dinner,
she peppers me with questions,
until she realizes
she won't get far.

She has Joseph drive her
to who knows where
and sometimes isn't back
until deep into the night.

Her fieldwork. When it comes
to zonbis,
the less I know,
the better.

Opportunity

Ever since the Fèt Gede,
it's as if Mamzelle herself
is possessed
by a spirit
that pushes her
to wake up early
and work hard
until late at night,
mainly in her room,

with less time
on her fieldwork.

One afternoon,
Mamzelle brings out her scrapbook
and asks me to sit next to her
on the parlor sofa,
where I never sit.

"I'm working on a novel
I've wanted to write
for a long time,"
she says.

"Let me show you
a few things
about my past."

She opens the scrapbook
on her lap. I'm surprised to see
how perfectly neat
the pages are.

"I grew up
in a town run by our own people,
like yours in Haiti,
where my father was a preacher
and a mayor. We had a big house
surrounded by trees.

"This is a photo
of Mama. She died
when I was thirteen."
Mamzelle turns the page
so quickly
all I see is a black-and-white blur

of a woman in white
and a man dressed in a suit.

"This is one of the first
poems I ever wrote. It's called 'Home.'
How do you say that in Kreyol?"

"Lakay,"
I respond,
thinking of Fifina's
book of recipes.

"Lakay," she repeats,
almost correctly.

She turns the page.

"This is when I graduated
from the best university
for our people, Howard."

Mamzelle wearing a black gown,
a flat square hat with a tassel,
with such a big smile,
it's contagious.

"One of the happiest days
of my life. But it wasn't easy
for me to get there.
I had to lie about my age
to be able to go
to the school that was free.

"After Mama died,
my father stopped paying
my school fees
when he met his new wife,

who was just a bit older than me.
But that's another story . . ."

Are Mamzelle's eyes
welling with tears?

She clears her throat.
"There were some tough years.
Eventually, I realized
if I wanted an education,
I'd have to
shave ten years off
my real age
to be able to go
to the free school.
I loved that school,
even though I had to work
all kinds of jobs
when I wasn't studying
to pay for everything I needed.
In the end, it was worth it.

"You do whatever you need
for freedom.
But I don't need
to tell a Haitian that."

Mamzelle laughs,
and I'm surprised when
I join her.

"This is one of the first
short stories I published,
and this is the award ceremony,
where I won the most awards."

She lingers on those photos.
One is the front page
of a magazine:
OPPORTUNITY.

"Does this mean the same in English,
as it does in French?" I ask.

"Yes, exactly. 'Opportunity' is like 'opportunité.'
It was one of the best magazines
our people ever created,
and when my stories were published there
and won prizes,
people sat up and took notice.
My life changed
almost overnight.

"It will change again
when this new novel
I'm writing here
gets published."

She's beaming now,
but she gently closes her scrapbook.

"That's enough for now.
I just wanted to show you
that I'm not like Katherine Dunham,
the toast of the town.
Or like Madame Ovide and her friends.

"Nothing
was ever handed to me."

Or to me.

When Mamzelle was young,
was she a shadow girl, too?
How did she get
from there to here?

DECEMBER 1, 1936

Uninvited

Mamzelle is
in the bedroom
clacking away
on her typewriter.

A sharp knock
at the front door.
Mamzelle didn't say
there'd be any visitors.

I straighten my mouchwa madras
on my head—
Mamzelle does not like
the stiff white cap
Madame Ovide had me wear—
and open the front door.

"Bonjour,"
says a wiry light-skinned man
dressed in a perfectly pressed
white linen suit.

It's Pince-Nez
from Madame's dinner party.

"I am here
to see Mademoiselle Hurston,"
handing me
his hat and his cane.

I tell him to wait
while I fetch Mamzelle,
who is never happy
when I interrupt
while she's working.

"Who is he?"

"I saw him once
at Madame Ovide's,
but I don't know his name.
He didn't offer it,
and he didn't give me
his calling card."

Mamzelle stubs out her cigarette,
spritzes perfume,
strides to the parlor.

"Good morning, Miss Hurston."

He bows, kisses her hand.

He must be high up
in the government.

What does he want
with Mamzelle?

Mamzelle lights a cigarette
and crosses her legs.

"So you've found me."

Mamzelle doesn't bother
asking his name.

She seems to know
exactly who he is.

Watched

"I simply wanted
to offer my *personal* welcome
to our beautiful country.

"You must know
we Haitians
are solicitous
of our guests,
especially those
who voyage from
such a great distance,
like yourself."

His French is too perfect,
all tight and polite
and sharp as
an ice pick.

"And you are indeed
a guest
in our country,"
he adds,
flicking a piece
of lint
from his knee.

He leans back
in the wicker chair,
pulls out a cigar.

"Would you like a drink?"
asks Mamzelle,
glancing over at me.

He ignores her offer
and puffs his cigar.

"I hear you've taken
a considerable interest
in the case of a poor woman,"
he says.

"Which woman
might that be?
There are many
poor women in Haiti."

"Mademoiselle Hurston,
let's not waste
any more time.
We know where you went
and where you plan to go."

"Really?
Word must travel fast
by teledjol. Isn't that the
right expression in Kreyol
for 'bush telegraph'?"

Mamzelle blows
her cigarette smoke
over her shoulder.

Pince-Nez crosses his legs,
his creases so perfect,
I have to hide my amazement.

"Ah, yes. You must mean
my coming appointment
with the esteemed Dr. Léon,
your director of public health,
who studied obstetrics
in Europe?"
asks Mamzelle.

"It gives me such pleasure
to know how closely you follow
my comings and goings.
Do all the guests in your country
get this kind of personal attention,
or am I just *lucky*?"

"I will take a drink,"
says Pince-Nez
without looking at me.

Fruitless

I go into the kitchen
and fetch the bottle of rum.

When I return,
Mamzelle's smoking a new cigarette
and tapping her fingers
on the arm of her chair.

"I'm afraid your interest
in that poor woman

will prove fruitless,"
says Pince-Nez. "There are
no zombies in Haiti,
despite what Mr. Seabrook wrote
in *The Magic Island*.
An atrocious book."

"I agree he packed it with lies,
says Mamzelle. "But, look,
the *White Zombie* film
is making Hollywood rich.

"Why wouldn't you welcome
a book with the truth?"

"All books and films about zombies
spread the dangerous lies
that are voodoo.
They are an insult to my people
and scare tourists away,"
says Pince-Nez.

I tighten my grip
on the tray. Is *this* really
what Mamzelle wants?

She pretends to care
about folk music
and proverbs.
She really wants
the secret of zonbis.
Then she'll write her *own* book
to make lots of money.

"If there are no zombies,
then why are you

so interested
in my research?"

Pince-Nez stands up
abruptly. I move
to put down the tray
and get his hat
but he holds up his hand.

"It's so warm. I'd like
a glass of coconut water."

"Lucille will get it for you."

But before she can say more,
he follows me
into the kitchen.
I know better
than to speak to him
first.

He stands
closely behind me
his hot cigar breath
burning into my neck

watching me move
as if he's afraid
I might poison him.

I slowly pour
the coconut water
from the pitcher.

He sees
the bottle of Barbancourt

and gestures
for some in his glass.

"I know who you are,"
he says,
gritting his teeth.

He takes a sip,
looks me up and down.

"Just like
the section chief's mother,
I don't forget faces."

> I'm frozen
> in place
> like my Venus ice sculpture
> he saw that evening.

"I'm sorry, but
you must be thinking
of someone else."

It takes everything I have
to control the tremble
in my voice.

"If you help me,
I can help you
find your friend."

Does he really know
where Fifina is?
How can I find out
without betraying Mamzelle?

"You must be thinking
of somebody else.
My face is so ordinary,
that happens a lot."

He places his glass
on the counter
and nods for more rum.

At Madame's dinner party,
Pince-Nez stared a hole
through Oreste
when he talked about
Vincent and Trujillo.

I steady my hand
as I pour.

Mamzelle's car
is pulling up now.
Joseph took it
to the garage.

He's back
just in time.

Eat You Up

When Joseph sees
Pince-Nez's car
parked on the street,
he doesn't get out
of the car, only rolls down
the window.

Pince-Nez tells me to wait in the kitchen,
then he goes outside.

From the open window,
I can hear his words clearly.

"Get out of the car.
Have you done
what I told you?"

There's no doubt Pince-Nez
enjoys giving orders.

Joseph gets out of the car
slowly
and leans away from Pince-Nez.

The two men stand tense
in the afternoon sun.

"Imbecile!"

Joseph's eyes
stay glued to the ground.

"Didn't I tell you
to keep an eye on her?
We want to know
where she goes,
who she sees.
Or else."

Pince-Nez makes a gun
with his finger,
points it at Joseph's head,
and whispers something I can't hear.

"Lucille!"

I nearly
knock over the bottle.

Mamzelle joins me
in the kitchen.

"What are they saying?"
she whispers.

"I can't hear it all,
but I know Joseph,
and he is afraid."

Mamzelle winces,
then straightens her back.

"I can tell you one thing,"
says Mamzelle.
"He's no friend
to people like me,
or anyone else
who doesn't go along
to get along."

When Pince-Nez
returns to the kitchen,
his mask is firmly
back in place.

"Your maid,"
he says, staring at me,
"was kind enough to
pour me rum
and coconut water."

Mamzelle's smile is tight
as she escorts him
back to the parlor.

"Haitian peasants
are such a poetical group,
don't you think?"
he says, raising his glass.

"What would Haiti be
without its rich folklore?
Haitian peasants
can be so easily
misunderstood
by people
who don't know them.
The Haitian peasant
has a classic expression:
'I'll eat you up
without any salt.'

"Yet of course,
they don't mean it literally."

Mamzelle sips her rum
and lets out a sigh.

"Don't worry, Miss Hurston.
We always
take *good* care
of our guests."

Mamzelle makes a sound
like agreement,
walks Pince-Nez to the door.

I hand him his hat.

His gets into his car
and drives away.

Joseph,
nowhere in sight.

Warning

Only when the car is long gone
do I ask Mamzelle his name.

"His name doesn't matter.
I've met people like him before."

"What kind of people?"

"He's probably from Vincent's
secret police.
He thinks I'm one of those
Americans who comes down here
to pick the bones
of your culture,
write a bunch of lies,
and make lots of money
doing it."

"What kind of lies?"

"The lies that keep tourists away.
Lots of white people
think Haiti is
a land of savages.
Hollywood loves making movies
with flesh-eating zombies,

devil worship,
and voodoo priests
sticking pins in dolls."

My shoulders tighten,
but I pull myself taller.

So that's how they see us.
We're not even human.

"Why would anyone
be afraid of us?"

"Other than the fact
that Haiti
freed itself from slavery?
That was scary enough!
Fear makes money.
Hollywood makes movies.
New York makes books.
They all want to make money."

I think of saying Oreste
is in New York,
but quickly decide
this isn't the time.

"Why does he want
to scare you?"
I ask her.

"So I won't tell the truth
about zombies."

"What *is* the truth?"

Mamzelle's fists rise,
as if she's ready to fight.

"Some people in power
use voodoo to control others.
It's complicated.
The less you know now,
the better.

"But with what I've been learning,
no one will hurt us."

Proverbs

She said "us."

But what did she learn
that could save us
from Pince-Nez
and the secret police?

His threats
lingered in the air.
Mamzelle tried her best
not to look rattled at dinner,
but for once,
she went to bed early.

The next morning after breakfast
Mamzelle asks me
to help translate some proverbs.

I sit down with her,
explain what they mean,

while Mamzelle
makes notes in English.

1. *Tout bèt jennen mòde!*
All beasts bite when they're cornered.

2. *Granmèsi chin se kout baton.*
Thanking the dog is a stroke of the stick.

3. *Rayi chin; di dan-li blanche.*
Hate the dog, but admit that his teeth are white.

4. *Chin grangou pa kouche.*
A hungry dog can't sleep.

5. *Se chin map leve pou-m kouche.*
I'm pushing dogs aside in order to lie down.

6. *Pote mak sonje kout baton.*
He who bears the scars remembers the stick.

7. *Ti Mapou pa grandi anba gwo mapou.*
A little mapou tree doesn't grow under a big mapou tree.

8. *Fèy mapou sanble ak fèy manyòk.*
Mapou leaves look like manioc leaves.

9. *Mapou tonbe, kabrit maje fèy li.*
The mapou tree falls; goats eat its leaves.

10. *Se kouto sèlman ki konnen sa ki nan kè yanm.*
Only the knife knows what's in the yam's heart.

She thanks me with a hug.

Says she understands
what all of them mean,
except the last one.

"I think it means
some secrets are better left alone,"
I offer.

And I want to add:

*That would be the best one
for you to remember.*

Questions

That afternoon I ask Joseph
what Pince-Nez whispered.

At first he lies
and says "Nothing."
Then he finally admits
that things are bad.

"They're ready to stop her,
whatever it takes."

"What do you mean,
'whatever it takes'?"

"These people are high up.
They can hurt us, and . . ."

"And *what*, Joseph?"

"Nothing. I can't say any more."
Joseph just shakes his head
and stares at his feet.

"I have a wife and a baby.
They are my life.
This is too much for me."

I know what it's like
to fear for your family.

How to stop Mamzelle
from getting us all
in trouble?

Mamzelle is only a guest.
She'll go back to her land,
but whatever she does
will stick to us
like hot tar on our heels.

And who knows just
how far *they* are willing to go?

As far as they went
with Fifina and her father?

I don't want that
for anyone.

All because Mamzelle
keeps asking questions
she shouldn't be asking.

Two Shadow Girls

That night,
as I turn down her bed,
Mamzelle stands at the door,
smoking.

"You know,
I did this work myself

when I was your age."
She observes me.

"I was only thirteen
when I left home.
Worked in all kinds of places.
Let me see your hands."

I hold them out,
    cringing inside.
I hope they felt softer
back when Oreste held them
on my way home from tasting ice.

"Just what I thought.
You need my special corn lotion.
It's a secret recipe
a black Seminole woman
taught me."

Mamzelle reaches
for a brown glass bottle
on her dressing table.

"Each year they
    do a Green Corn Dance.
They stomp around
a big fire all night,
    singing and praying.
By the end, I was so tired,
I fell asleep right there on the ground,
felt the earth breathing in and out."

Mamzelle rubs the rough patches
where the calluses are.

"It was hard at that age,
especially with men
old enough to be my daddy.
One offered to take me to Canada.
His wife
got wind of the plan
and I got the boot.

"But at least
I kept one of his beautiful books.
Paradise Lost."

I close my eyes,
smell the wood pulp and leather
of Oreste's books.

I open them
to find Mamzelle
staring at my palm.

"The life line is long, but the love line . . ."

"What?"

Mamzelle holds up her palm
and traces the broken brown curve
from above the thumb.

"It's broken."

"What does that mean?"

"Don't worry.
It's the same with me."

Birthdays

Tomorrow is my birthday.
Last year,
my entire world was a different place.
When I turned sixteen,
Papa gave me my mother-of-pearl-
handle knife

and Fifina,
she gave me
a day I will never forget.

It was my fifth birthday
that Papa taught me to swim.

I was afraid
of the waterfall caves,
afraid of dark cliffs
underwater.

"This was one
of your mother's favorite places."

He held me up lightly;
my legs and arms paddled.

I was afraid
of deep-water monsters
grabbing my ankles
dragging me down.

"I'm right here.
Swim into my arms."

I kept paddling forward

until with one final leap

I reached him.

Turning Seventeen

No one to celebrate
my seventeenth birthday.

I didn't tell Mamzelle,
who is rushing around excited
to welcome her special visitor.

Joseph, with his twitchy mustache,
is picking him up
from his hotel
and driving him over.

"He's a friend from America
here to help me
research your country's folk music.
We've worked together before.
I even had to sweet-talk him
out of jail once!"

I hardly hear her. Instead,
my heart softens as I hear Oreste
playing "Ti Zwazo"
our last evening together.
Is that folk music, too?

"Please make a special lunch
for Monsieur Alan Lomax."

I had decided on lambi with pikliz
and diri ak djons djons.

I'd woken up before dawn,
to pound the lambi,
marinate it in lime sauce,
make the pickled
pepper sauce,
and soak the black mushrooms
for the long-grain rice.

When Joseph drives me
to the Iron Market, which I insist
has better choices for Mamzelle,
I take my time. No more Celestina
to rush me. I'm so relieved
I haven't bumped into her
yet.

To anyone willing, I show
my drawing of Fifina. I already left
two copies with Madan Sara, gave
Cousin Phebus two copies,
and kept three for myself.
Oreste's gift swells my heart.

"Have you seen this girl?"

"Se yon bèl marabou," they all say,
but none say they've seen her.

Mamzelle's Special Friend

It's already noon
when Mamzelle's special friend arrives.
He's a young white man,
the first white man I've met.

His thick brown hair frames
a face without whiskers,
a mouth that speaks gently.

He reminds me
of Oreste.

He sets a big
leather suitcase
carefully on the floor.

"What's your name?"

His French is much better
than Mamzelle's.

"Lucille."

"Want to take a look?"

He opens
the leather case.
I peer in.

It's bigger
than Madame's gramophone.

"This is where
we ask people to sing."
He holds a metal tube
to his mouth.

"This is where
the needle writes
your voice
on the record."

He shows me
an aluminum disc
and the special needles
that he says will etch
the sound onto it.

He takes one already made
from inside its brown paper sleeve.

It's black and shiny
with tiny grooves on it,
like the rings of a tree.

He sets up a shiny
silver-colored microphone,
large stripes on its head,
and asks me to stand near it.

"Want to say something
into the microphone?"

I glance at Mamzelle,
who nods.

"Bonjou, tout moun.
Mwen rele Lucille."

I can't think of anything better
than saying my name.

"And my name is Alan.
Now your voice
will live forever.

"This is the recorder
I use for my fieldwork,"
he says.
"You could call me
a song hunter."

"A bit like what I do
with stories,"
says Mamzelle.

"We both go poking our noses
into people's lives
to save something precious
they don't always know they have,"
she adds.

I'm hardly listening—
my head is spinning with joy.

*My voice will have wings
and travel the world.*

Latibonit O

This morning Mamzelle
asked me to press
her cherry-red dress
of silk
that matches
her lipstick.
She even asked me

to help curl her hair
with pomade
and the flat iron.

Now she sits smoking,
crosses and uncrosses
her bare legs.

"Thanks for buying me the stockings
I asked for. You got it just right:
size ten, light tan,"
she says to Mesye Lomax.

She holds them up
to the sunlit window,
caressing them.
Madame Ovide
had stockings like that.

They both laugh,
but I find it strange
that a white man
would buy stockings
for Mamzelle.

Her voice sounds lighter,
like a girl in love sounds.

I should know.

It only lowers
when he mentions
that his fiancée
will be joining him next month.

"So soon? Please give her my best.
More rum?"

Mesye puts his hand
over his glass.

"Zora, are you trying
to get me drunk? It wouldn't be
the first time!"

They laugh again,
like they have shared adventures
in the past.

"You never used to mind,"
she says, her mouth a mock pout.
"Are you already a married man?"

He shakes his head, smiling.

"I'm so grateful
for everything you've done,
all the letters of introduction.
Thank you!"

"Anything for you,
my friend,"
says Mamzelle,
but I can easily
imagine her
replacing
that last word
with "love."

"Lucille, is there
any song
you want to sing?"
he asks,

Surprised,
I glance at Mamzelle.

"Go ahead. This is
your time to shine.
Alan is collecting Haiti's
folk songs
for the Library of Congress.
That's America's
biggest library."

I don't know what
that kind of library
could look like. Maybe like
the Mission School's,
only much bigger.
A cathedral
of bright leather books,
like Oreste's,
that reach from floor to ceiling.

I picture everything bigger
in America.

That's all very nice,
but not why
I want to sing today.

It's my birthday,
and this is a gift
I can give myself.

I close my eyes
and remember.
Manman   Papa
Mapou   Cousin Phebus

Sister Gilberte   Tante Lila
the famn lakou

Fifina. My sixteenth.
Her gift. The cave.
Running hand in hand.
The kiss.

Oreste. Dous lèt.
Our outside life.
Tasting ice.
Our slow-burn kiss.
The memory of water.

Ti Zwazo.

Only my voice
can nest all these birds
when I sing.

    "Latibonit O
     yo voye rele mwen
     Yo dim Soley malad
      Soley malad li kouche.

    "Latibonit O
     yo voye rele mwen
     Yo dim Soley malad

    "Le m te rive
     mwen jwenn Soley kouche
     Le m te rive
     mwen jwenn Soley mouri

    "Kisa poum fe O
     poum antere Soley

Mwen di kisa poum fe O
poum antere Soley

"Sa fèm lapenn O
Pou'm antere Soley
Se regretan
sa pou'm antere."

> Latibonit O,
> they sent me word
> the sun was sick
> and lying still.
>
> Latibonit O,
> they sent me word
> the sun was sick.
>
> When I arrived,
> I found the sun lying still.
> When I arrived,
> I found the sun had died.
>
> What could I do?
> How could I bury the sun?
> I say what could I do?
> How could I bury the sun?
>
> It made me sad to bury the sun,
> I felt so sorry to bury the sun.

"Beautiful!" Mesye Alan's eyes shine
as he translates my words.

Mamzelle puts out her cigarette.

"Well done! That's just what we needed.

"Now we'd better
get down to business
and record
some of my songs."

She steps up
to the microphone,
taking my place.

"Thank you, Lucille.

"Please have lunch ready
on the veranda in an hour."

Even the chill in her words
can't bury my birthday sun.

Drums in the Night

The drums begin talking
somewhere high in the hills.

Mamzelle has already been
to see many temples,
to meet houngans and mambos
for her book. She even says
she was initiated into hoodoo
in New Orleans.

Good for her.
But what are these drums?
It's not Carnival yet.

These drumbeats are different.
Mamzelle will want to see them,
even in the middle of the night.

It's hard to fall asleep
when I hear Mamzelle
pacing, not snoring,
next door.

Mamzelle isn't one
to walk in her sleep.
When I hear her
knock at my door,
I'm not surprised.

"Get dressed. We're going out."

"Now? Where are we going?"

"To find
those rada drums."

I pretend to yawn,
rubbing sleep from my eyes.

"What's rada?" I pretend not to know,
hoping it will
at least slow her down.

Mamzelle taps her feet.

"Something special.
Hurry up!"

She holds a lantern,
her canvas bag
with red notebook
and camera.

How can I stop her,
for her own good?

Stopping Mamzelle

How can I stop Mamzelle
from going out to the drums?

I move slowly
to give myself time.

I step carefully into
the leather sandals
Papa made
and fiddle with the ankle straps.

"Come on, Lucille!"

Mamzelle is standing
at the front door.

There's only one thing
I can do. I grab
Mamzelle's arm
and pull her back in.

Mamzelle is so surprised,
she stands like Lot's wife.

"What the hell are you doing?"
she asks, freeing her arm.

She sounds more hurt
than angry.
At least that's a start.

We stand face-to-face.

Mamzelle's eyes flash questions.
"Don't tell me you're afraid

of going out in the dark?
Or is it the drums?"

I remain silent,
unmoving.

Let Mamzelle think what she wants.
Let her kick me out
right now

as long as she doesn't
step foot outside tonight.

"You don't want to go, fine!
But get out of my way,
because I'm going
to find those rada drums."

I remain standing.
I close my eyes.

"Do not search for the drums,"
I say quietly.

"Now, look, Lucille,
this is exactly the research
I need for my book.
This is why
they paid me to come."

"Who paid you?"

"People with lots of money
who help people like me
write books."

Her words will not move me.

"Do *not* search for the drums."

"Why?"

"Because sometimes my dreams
turn out to be true."

Mamzelle stares hard
at the door, then at me.

"And you dreamed
something bad would happen
to me?"

My nod is a whisper.

May Bondye forgive me
for this white lie
that can protect us all.

"Last night,
I dreamed
if you went to the drums,
you would be in danger."

Mamzelle backs down
and takes off her coat.
She sighs long and hard.

"We'll do it your way,
for now."

Her words float
in the darkness.
But I can tell she trusts me.

She goes to her room.

Late into the night,
her typewriter keys
clack-clack in time
to the drums.

To Save Her

The next morning,
Mamzelle asks
for breakfast
on the terrace.

I bring her coffee
with the red sugar
she loves.

"Mèsi, Lucille."

Mamzelle takes a sip
and sighs.

"I know you
don't serve the spirits
and don't want to learn
about them,
but even you must know
the Fèt Gede
is special.

"Maybe that's why
last night
I dreamed
of my mother,"
she says.

I put down
my cleaning cloth
and sit at the table.

Mamzelle never
talks about her dreams.

"My mother's name
was Lucy,
and she died
when I was young."

I lean closer.

"I stayed by her bed
as she got sicker.
I read poems to her.
One of her favorites
was a poem called
'If'
by a man named
Rudyard Kipling.

"I know it by heart.
This part was the best:

"'If you can make one heap of all your winnings
And risk it on one turn of pitch-and-toss,
And lose, and start again at your beginnings
And never breathe a word about your loss . . .'

"I told her
the day I risk it all
it's to win, not to lose!

"That made her laugh.
I loved hearing her laugh."

Now I understand
why Mamzelle
laughs so loud.

"I recited the whole story
of Demeter and Persephone,
my favorite myth.

"I told her I would turn
it around. Why *couldn't*
a daughter save
her mother?"

The Pillow and the Clock

"I fed her myself,
spooned her soup,
mashed bananas and porridge,"
says Mamzelle.

"Nothing helped.
She grew weaker and weaker.

"She asked me to read
from the Bible,
the Book of Psalms."

Mamzelle pushes her coffee away,
takes out a cigarette,
breathes in deep and long.

"Then one day
when her voice was
so weak, I could hardly hear her,
she said,

"'Don't let them
take the pillow
from under my head.

"'Don't let them
cover the clock.'"

I understand
Mamzelle's mother.

Taking the pillow away
makes it easier for death
to come.

Covering the clock
means she wouldn't
stop time when she died.

Mamzelle's mother
was not ready to die.

"My family gathered around
that night, and the doctor
held a mirror to her mouth.

"Papa started taking
the pillow away.

"I screamed and tried to stop them.
I pleaded and cried, but they all held me back.

"Then I heard the last rasping,
and I knew Mama was gone."

"What could you do?
You were only a girl."
I say these words softly.

Mamzelle's eyes
well with tears.

"I should have done what she asked me to do.
In my dream last night, she told me,

"I've always wanted
to bring back the dead.

"Maybe that's
the real reason I want
the secret of zombies."

Now I understand.

She misses her mother,
just like I do.
But she'll get us in trouble
if she keeps up this digging.

DECEMBER 15, 1936

For Strong Emotions

It's been exactly one year
since I lost Fifina.

A day I wish
never existed.

I wake up feeling
like I want to throw up.

My whole body aches,
sinking low
into the ground.

Would Fifina's
Recipe for Strong Emotions
really help me,
unlike the one for
a Cracked Heart?
It's been so long
since I've tried.

> Make an infusion from three leaves
> of purple verbena.
> Steep it for three days.
>
> On the fourth day,
> take two big spoonfuls
> of the juice of these leaves.
>
> Mix it with
> palma Christi castor oil
> and a spoonful of
> leftover coffee essence
> from the bottom of the cup.
>
> Drink it
> as a purge.

Of course
I will try it,
though it's not
strong emotions
that I need
a recipe for.

Driving Herself

Later that morning,
Mamzelle asks me
to come with her
on an errand.

Joseph is nowhere
to be found.
"He asked for time off
to visit his family.
Didn't say for how long.
Not a problem for me!
I like driving
myself much better
than being a passenger."

Mamzelle whistles,
takes curves in the road
a little too fast.
Her camera bag
shifts in her lap.

"Where are we going?"

"To meet someone special."

The Hospital

We pull up to a big hospital.

Why does Mamzelle need a doctor?

At the front desk, Mamzelle
straightens her back.
"I have an appointment

with Dr. Legros.
The director of public health,
Dr. Léon, arranged it for me."

Her voice fills the room.
The woman at the desk nods,
gets up, and walks briskly
down the hall.

Sweat prickles
my upper lip.
"Why are we here?"

"I told you. If I can discover
the truth about zombies,
it will help people around the world,"
says Mamzelle, her voice rising
with excitement.

We need to leave here.
As soon as we can.

Dr. Legros is light-skinned like Madame,
but his face is round and kind.
He leads us into an open courtyard.

"I'd be surprised
if you get anywhere,
Miss Hurston.

"This is a secret
passed along from family to family
since nan Guinée."

Secrets from Africa,
first home of the ancestors,

where only the knife
knows the heart of the yam.

"Lucille, will you come with me to the yard,
where I will take some photographs?"

"Can't you do that by yourself?"
I ask her, almost pleading.

"What are you afraid of?
You don't serve the spirits,
do you?" asks Mamzelle.

"Maybe we all serve them,
one way or another," I answer.

"Then you're a believer?"
she says.

"Maybe,
in some ways, I am."

"Lucille, I didn't go after the drums
when you asked me not to.

"But I really need this photograph.
It could make my career.
If you help me now,
I promise I'll help you, too."

Maybe, with those rich white people
she knows, Mamzelle can help me
find Fifina. She can offer a reward
for information.

And then she'll take us with her
to New York,
to find Oreste.

In a Corner

My love.
The sun in my heart
is waking again.

I agree to help Mamzelle.

In the hospital courtyard,
Dr. Legros points to a crouched woman
in the farthest corner.

Her head is covered with a cloth,
and she is sweeping the ground
with a bare branch,
like the ones I used
when I was a little girl,
drawing birds
in the red earth.
She's curled tight like a dog
afraid to be hit.

"Felicia Felix-Mentor
is from Ennery,"
says Dr. Legros
as we make our way
to her corner.
"It's a town
between Gonaïves
and Cap-Haïtien.

"She helped her husband
with their grocery store.

"They had no children.
The husband was cruel.

One day, she suddenly
got sick.
People say
she was buried
near her house.

"The years passed.
The husband remarried,
became a top civil servant
with his new wife's efforts.

"Then one day,
nearly thirty years
after Felicia's burial,
she was found
naked on a farm,
insisting it was her father's.

"You can imagine
how this frightened the tenants,
who chased her away.

"They finally called in
the section chief,
who reported the case
to the national police.

"Even though
her own brother
recognized her,
after all those years,
no one wanted
anything to do with her,
which is how
she ended up here."

Her Face Was Covered

Mamzelle's already
taking pictures
with her camera,
which hangs from a leather strap
around her neck.

She tells me it's a new camera,
so light
that war photographers can use it
to take photos in battle,
as they are now doing
in Spain,
where General Franco
is getting help from the Germans
to fight the resistance.

What would Fifina's father
write about that?
Is he even still alive?

I fight to keep
the bile from rising
into my throat.

When Dr. Legros approaches,
Felicia starts trembling.

"These ladies won't hurt you.
They've only come
to take your picture."

Felicia keeps her face covered
with a rough piece of burlap.

Mamzelle adjusts her tripod.
"Lucille, come help me."

I don't know what help
she wants, but I do know
that we need to *leave*.
Now.

Close-Up

Dr. Legros asks Felicia
to uncover her face.
She flinches.

"Don't be afraid.
No one will hurt you,"
says Dr. Legros.

"Is she *really* a zonbi?"
I turn to Mamzelle.

"Some old people still say
your soul can be stolen
if your picture is taken."

        "Her soul was stolen
         a long time ago.

        "Telling her story
         is the best we can do."

After more coaxing
from Dr. Legros and Mamzelle,
Felicia uncovers her face.

I hold my breath
when I see her eyes.
They're nearly all white,
with pink around the rims.

Her thick graying hair
is cut short,
her skin dusty
but smooth.

What things has she seen
in those thirty years?

I remember
the boy in chains
and make
the sign of the cross.

Mamzelle's still
taking pictures.

"Where are you from?"
Dr. Legros asks me.

"Near Hinche."

"Hmm. There was a young woman
from there
brought in
a few weeks ago.

"There were
two women
helping her.

"The well-dressed woman
seemed to know

Dr. Sam, our head of obstetrics,
very well. He was the one
who took care of the girl.
There aren't many places
that will help girls
in her condition."

Fifina?

"What was her name?"

"I didn't catch it."

I pull out my drawing
and show him.

"Well,
she looked more disheveled,
but, yes, that looks like her.
She'd lost
so much blood,
she got here just in time."

Blood?

"What happened to—
to the girl?"
I manage to stutter,
fear damming my voice.

"We managed to save her,
but not her baby."

A tidal wave of nausea
knocks me to the ground.

Felicia in My Dreams

When you see dry bones by the side of the road, don't forget they used to be flesh and blood. Don't know how I survived. Bondye must have spared me for a reason. My husband grew tired of beating me day after day after he realized my womb would never bear children. So he went to see a bocor. One minute I was eating dinner in the courtyard, alone. Next minute I knew I was waking up in a cane field, alone. Couldn't remember what happened. Didn't know where I was. Had to beg in the street to survive. Mainly on the church steps. Sometimes on the big road to the capital. My eyes look so strange because I've seen so much death. I was on the road that day when a bus drove by. People stared out the window at me, a few with pity. To them I was just an old woman begging in the road, no family, no home. The sun was shining through the rain. The devil was beating his mother. He was laughing at her tears. Perhaps she knew what was coming. Then I heard the driver shout, the bus bounced off rocks, screams, whimpers, moans, prayers. Smelled rubber, metal, humans, all burning together. Stood up and saw fire licking everything black at the bottom of the cliff. Smoke stung my eyes, never the same. People will see my photo and think they know who I am. Wrong, just like fanm Ameriken sa. She thought I was a zonbi from the land of the dead. Wrong. I lost my life, but I didn't die. Like your friend. If the fanm Ameriken keeps making trouble, they'll kill her, like my husband tried to kill me. At least I'm safe here. When your friend came, she was weak and bleeding. Two women helped carry her in. She said she was running away from a gwo zouzoun who made her his outside wife. He promised to keep her father alive if she stayed with him. She read his letters in secret and found out her father was dead. Maybe that's what killed her baby. When your friend lost the baby, she said she was going to a place no one could find her. I think I heard Cazales. Death always finds a way in even when all the doors are locked. And people wonder what my eyes are watching. When you see dry bones by the side of the road, don't forget they used to be flesh and blood.

Between

That morning I started my own
days of blood. Without a cloth
or safety pins, I had to ask
Mamzelle for help.

"This is your first period?"
I nod, still feeling queasy.

"Are you all right?
Do you need anything?"

After yesterday's surprise,
she seems more ready to help.

"I have some Kotex.
Let me show you
how to use them.
Do you have clean panties?"

I go into my room
and bring them out.

We go into the bathroom.
"Wash the blood with this."
She hands me a wet washcloth.
I wash the warm stickiness
without looking down.
My insides are cramping
so much I double over.

Mamzelle helps me to the bathtub
and runs the tap to fill it.

"Take a hot bath now. I'm putting in
some Epsom salts. That's what I use.

I'll go get you an aspirin
for the cramps. I used to get those
every month. Now it's less often."

When she leaves, I undress
and slip into the tub.

Mamzelle returns, holding up
a white rectangle of cotton
attached to an elastic belt.

My own days of blood
have begun.
Another prayer
not answered

The Bride Specialist

Mamzelle sits by the side
of the claw-foot
porcelain tub
while I let myself
soak in warm water
up to my chin.
My first bath
like this.

"I know with this bleeding
and the pain you're in,
your body
feels like a burden.

"Some people
will even want to make
it a mule.

"Don't let them."

"What do you mean?"

I'm thinking of
Cousin Phebus
and Fifina,
whose bodies
brought them
nothing but trouble.

That's why I wanted
to never start bleeding.

And then, of course,
the Sisters warned us
about mortal sin,
concupiscence,
and adultery.

The body makes us
vulnerable
to the desires of men.

The flesh makes men
weak, they said.

"When I was in Jamaica,"
Mamzelle says,
"I went to stay
with the Maroons
in a place called Accompong."

"Like the mawons
who escaped into the
mountains and used a lambi shell
to call others to freedom?"

I ask.
"My great-grandfather
did that."

"Yes, like him,"
she responds.

"When a young woman
was ready for marriage,
there was an old woman
who'd prepare her.

"She was called
the bride specialist.

"I watched her
bathe a young virgin
in a secret mix of herbs
and massage her
with lemon and verbena oil."

That's not a recipe
Fifina has in her book.

"The bride specialist
showed her
the best ways to make love
with a man."
Mamzelle sighs.

"I'm guessing you've never
been with a boy."

"Not that way.
Kissing, yes, but—"

I stop myself.
This is already
too much to share.

"Did you ever
want to have children?" I ask her,
surprised at myself.
It must be the warm water
relaxing my body
and mind.

I could imagine
Oreste would be
a wonderful father.

I have no idea
what I'd be like
as a mother
since I never once had
my own mother with me.

"I had an operation
from a burst appendix."
She lifts up her shirt
and points to a ravine of a scar
on the right of her belly.

"There was an infection
and I nearly died
and had complications,
so I can't have children.

"But, yes, I like children.
Most people do, don't they?
Let me finish my story."

Mamzelle continues:
"Minutes before the wedding,
she gave the bride-to-be
a long sip of rum
steeped in ganga,
and she whispered
'Remember,
your body
is made
for love
and comfort.'

"I'll never forget
that night.
And I want you to
imagine that pleasure,
just for yourself.

"You don't need to be
a bride
to feel this good.

"Give your body
the love and comfort
it deserves.

"I interviewed
a peasant woman
who had moved to the city;
she said,
'Kò mwen se tè mwen'—

"my body is my land.

"Decide
how you'll plant it.

"You can
make it a garden
with pear trees
that blossom
with springtime
delight . . ."

Her voice trails off.

I close my eyes.

My body,
my land,
of birds and mapous,
and black butterflies
that grow strong
in the sun.

Becoming

No dreams
that night.
Or the next.

Just a week
of blood, cramps,
and throwing out
the soaking Kotex.
You don't wash these,
like Fifina had to.

"Just put them
in this burlap bag,"
said Mamzelle.

"I'll throw them out
with the trash."

Mamzelle is very
matter-of-fact
about the days of blood.
No stories of the moon
and tide
singing in my body,
like Fifina's mother.

In a strange way,
I like how
she makes it feel
ordinary.

"It's just part
of being a woman,"
she says.
"To me, it's not
the best part, but in many cultures,
there are ceremonies
to mark it."

She has the good sense
not to ask me if there's one here.

I wouldn't want any ceremony,
I just want
this pain to be over.

Pain, the famn lakou said,
is part of being a woman.

The Bible says it, too.

Days of blood.

Now I can make a baby.
And lose it, like Fifina.

Would having a baby
hurt this much?
Or kill me,
as it killed Manman?

There's no way
I want to find out.

Now I see why we say
women are the poto mitan.
We not only
hold up the temple;
we can also
hold up the sky.

Gazelle

I move slowly now,
like a sleepwalker.

The fog in my mind
muffles all sounds
and makes the world
a quiet, gray place.

> *Fifina's alive,*
> *but her baby died.*

> *Fifina's* alive,
> *but her baby* died.

> Fifina's *alive,*
> *but her* baby *died.*

Is Fifina like Felicia,
chained by death in life?

At least after seven days,
my bleeding stopped.
But it feels
like my body
has changed
in just one week.

I take another bath
in the bathtub,
for the second time
in my life.

The bliss
of letting my legs
float up,
then submerging my head
and holding my breath,
pretending I'm swimming
with Papa and Fifina.

When I look at myself
in the bathroom mirror,
I still see a gazelle,
thank goodness.

But I've changed. More swelling
in my breasts
the shape of half lemons,
and tufts of hair
between my legs.

There wasn't a mirror
for me to use
at Madame Ovide's.

I like that there's one here.

A Pilgrimage

On her way home
for Christmas and the holidays,
Cousin Phebus
comes to see me
at Mamzelle's.
Mamzelle is out,
so we sit on the veranda,
looking down on
the lush green, blue, and white
of the hills above the capital.

A shared moment,
a rare moment
of peace.

"I'm sorry I missed
your birthday. But here's
your father's gift, and
something from me."

I open Papa's burlap.
The ebony glows
dark and brilliant.
"What a beautiful piece!"

It makes me
want to reach for my knife.

"Yes, he knew
this birthday, your first away,
would be hard.

"The good news is
we convinced the police
that you've always heard voices,
had visions and dreams,
that you ran away
from home,
like such
a crazy girl would.

"The best Christmas gift
you could get.

"And this one
is from me."

She hands me a magazine.
It's the September issue
of *La Voix des Femmes*.
On its cover
is a massive fortress
on a hill overlooking the sea.

La Citadelle.

"Thank you, cousin! This is where
Mamzelle and I will be traveling
after the holidays."

"Then you're in luck.
Read this,

and you'll see why."
I take the magazine,
the first of my own,
and give her a kiss.

"I wrote down
my special recipe
for soupe joumou, since I know
you'll be making it
for Mamzelle."

She doesn't have much time
to stay, because the bus
will be coming by soon,
and she'll be heading home
for Christmas.

"Are you all right?"
she asks
at the door.

I'm looking down
at my feet, about to cry.
"I started bleeding."

"Ah, Ti Cousine. I thought
something was different."
She comes back
and hugs me tight.

"Did it hurt?"

"Yes."

"How long did it last?"

"Seven days."

She hugs me again.
"You're a woman now.
You know what that means.
If you ever make a baby,
I'll be the godmother."

"I don't think I want
to make a baby."

"Why not?"

"Because."

"You're afraid?"

"Yes."

"I understand.
I miss your mother, too.
I wish I had a choice
but now I don't. You still do.
Just make sure it's your choice."

"Mamzelle doesn't have children."

"Neither does Jeanne Perez."

We look at each other,
and suddenly we're giggling.

"They both seem fine.
They're not witches or hags,"
she says.

"We're all mothers, aunties, godmothers
in some way. We are mothering
every day. Not all of us
will be blessed with a baby,"

she adds, with only a hint
of sadness in her voice.

"You know, Ti Cousine,
everywhere I go, I show
your picture of Fifina.
We won't stop until we find her.
I meant to ask
how you got the copies
of your drawing."

"Oreste made them for me.
His father's friend
runs a printing press."

"Ooh," she says, smiling.
"So your little prince
is a good man after all."

"Not *all* men are pigs."

We laugh, hugging.
It feels good to laugh,
to know that we still have
our own sun inside us,
no matter how hard
some people try
to cloud it over.

It is ours,
and it still shines.

"Take good care of yourself,"
she says.
"Enjoy your pilgrimage.
Make some drawings for me.

I want to see what you saw
and hear every detail.

"I can't believe you'll be in all
the places where our history was made.
You'll be walking
in the ancestors' footsteps!

"Do you know
how lucky you are?"

This time when she says it,
my heart answers yes.

DECEMBER 22, 1936

Their Eyes

"I finished my novel
three days ago.
My Christmas gift to myself
is this trip to La Gonâve!"

I'm packing for Mamzelle's
five-day trip
to the island
not too far from us.

When she asked
if I wanted to join her,
I said, "No, thank you. I don't
want to miss my monthly
visit from my cousin,
especially since this will be

my first Christmas away
from home."

Mamzelle doesn't need to know
Phebus already came.

For the first time
in my life,
I will have a whole house
all to myself.

And I can't wait.

"I wrote it in seven weeks,
but it's been inside me
much longer,
waiting to be born.

"I put in it all of myself
and my love for a certain
young man I had to leave behind in
New York. My title is
Their Eyes Were Watching God."

I was only half listening
to Mamzelle's bubbling voice,
until I heard the word *love.*

Mamzelle was in love
and left him behind?

"Why?"
I ask her.

"Because it's a great title!
Don't you think? Oya,
the god of storms . . ."

"No, Mamzelle.
I meant
why did you leave
the man you loved?"

"Oh. Well, to make
a long story short,
he made my heart
and body sing,
in all the ways
I'd always dreamed of,
but he wanted a wife
who would give up her work.

"That's not me. If I couldn't write
and do my fieldwork,
I'd lose
what makes me me.

"No man is worth that."

Oreste would never
tell me to stop carving.
And if he ever did,
I'd know he wasn't
the man I think he is.

Love should spread joy,
not steal it.

DECEMBER 24, 1936

Christmas Eve Day

It feels like a lifetime ago
that I was with Cousin Phebus
as she prepared
our réveillon
Christmas Eve feast
we always ate after midnight Mass.

Instead, I'm alone
in Mamzelle's rented house.
Sitting on the veranda
reading *La Voix des Femmes*.

Another first.
I'm reading our history
written by Haitian women.

A history
I hardly knew existed.

Jeanne's Letter

I read the magazine
breathing in
the sweet scent
of ylang-ylang,
my whole body soothed
by the trees and flowers
that surround me.

No, it's not the same
as hearing Mapou's song

when I was back home.
But there's a song
I can listen to here,
when I have the silence
to hear it.

Jeanne's article
is called "A Pilgrimage"
and is written in the form
of a letter to her
four-year-old niece,
Madeleine Price-Mars,
part of that grande famille.

But really,
it's to all of us.

What sinks deep
into my skin
is what she says
about why
we should all
visit the Citadel
and Sans-Souci Palace,
both   cracked   wounded   abandoned,
where Henri Christophe,
who crowned himself king,
had his ill-fated reign.

Because,
unlike the common moth,
which is burned by the light,
we are like
our own Haitian butterflies,
with their brown-black wings,

that fly
in the dark of night
toward their home
of light,
where we recharge ourselves,
growing stronger.

Silent Day

All through the night
I read and reread,
drifting in and out
of a happy sleep.

At dawn, I stretch,
slowly eat a mango
on the veranda.

My favorite time
of day

when the world
holds its breath.

I have feasted
on a banquet
of words,
all the articles
in *La Voix des Femmes.*

Thank you, dear cousin.

As the sun sets,
my first Christmas alone,

I vow that
I will heed Jeanne's letter,
and open myself
to the ancestors.

I will find Fifina
and keep her safe,
something I could not do
for my own cousin.

I miss Fifina even more,
because in my bones I know
she is alive
and she must be found.

At least she's not
an ocean away,
like Oreste.

Tonight the sunset
blazes orange and gold.

For the first time
I can savor its light,
in silence,
alone.

DECEMBER 26, 1936

Her Scrapbook

When I was cleaning up
to prepare
for Mamzelle's return,
dusting her room,

I decided to peek
in the leather scrapbook
she'd shown me.

What she didn't show me
was what she'd written
on the very first page:

For Mama

Just two words.

She was collecting
all this evidence
of her success

for her mother,
whom she hoped
was watching
with pride.

Those two words
break the dam
of my tears.

My body shakes
as I sob
until the hurricane
inside has stripped
bare my land.

That night,
my dream is
one of the clearest
I've ever had.

Mamzelle, Dying

They want to stamp my passport and send me right over. Just because I had a stroke doesn't mean I'm ready. I still have something in my head for anyone who wants to listen. Never mind all my memories. I've been down before. When you see those dry bones by the side of the road, don't forget they used to be flesh and blood.

Sometimes they act like we're already dead. They clean up after us, all right, but their touch is rushed and distant. I used to be too proud to ask for help. Now I wish someone would rub my hands and read the story in my palms. Instead, eyes look away and fade into silence. All I see are dust motes, drenched in light. They kept me company for a while.

The red ball of the sun slides down the earth's belly. Still shines through the rain. "The devil is beating his mother." I remember when I wrote that one down in my notebook. It was in Haiti, all those years ago. The sun is the devil laughing; the rain is his mother's tears. I thought I was the expert, but it was Lucille who helped me understand. Never found the right place to use it until today.

Now I can see my firstborn. Seems like yesterday. My name in print, so long ago. I felt like Thor with his magic hammer, thunder roaring from his chariot. He was always my favorite.

My books were love letters to the world. With each one, I tried to catch God's attention. I wrapped a rainbow around my shoulders. Of course, back then I didn't know what I know now. Too impatient. Just wanted to step right through history's gates. Didn't know how much drifting I would do. One of those old Greeks said the art of living is learning how to die. Took me this long.

I used to be afraid of dying alone. Not anymore. Right now, I can see all my babies crowding around my bed: the ones I loved, like Janie and Tea Cake, and the ones who drove me to distraction, like Herod the Great. I gave them their wings, just like Mama gave me mine. Mama, watching from the chair in the corner. The day she died, my wanderings began. I know she'll cover the mirror for me.

Maybe these people feel sorry for me, but they don't see what I see. They see an old colored woman broken down, with a mysterious disease in her gut she says she got in a land where the dead come back to life. No husband, no children. At least a brother came to visit with his family.

A charity case. Crazy woman covers her bald patch with an old felt hat but still talks like she has the world on a string. Her hem unraveling tells another story. There was a time, I want to say, when I was known up and down Manhattan for my dazzling style.

These bones were flesh and blood.

They can't help steering clear. They're waiting until I die so they can cover me up like a bad mistake and pretend I was never here. Poor old lady.

But they're the poor ones—if only they knew!

There I am, back in Eatonville, sitting on the gatepost, asking everyone on the road if I can go with them.

I thought I was a woman in charge of my own destination.

Long before any of them could imagine me, I decided the world was my oyster and was too busy sharpening my knife to spend all my time talking about the thousand slights and humiliations, the self-hatred. I said no to these and other ways of dying.

No way would I be a slave ship in shoes.

When I sat alone in that hospital, I made a bet. I thought I had done nothing with my life so far, so no one would miss me. Nothing to lose. I promised that if I lived, I would be in charge of my journey, even if it meant I would travel alone.

No one held my hand as they wheeled me into the operating theater, flooded white with light. Mask over my mouth, falling backward into darkness.

My eyes were closed, but they were watching you.

When I woke up, I knew I had to keep my promise. I traveled on my own down South, toting a pistol and driving Sassy Susie, posing as a bootlegger to keep trouble at bay. From the backwoods of Florida to Baltimore, DC, Harlem, all on my own. A woman like you is asking for trouble. That didn't stop me. Then Jamaica, Haiti, and Honduras, only to return back where I began.

They said life left boot marks on my face. But they're wrong.

I faced down those mobs that accused me of molesting that landlady's boy. A lie so ugly I wanted to die.

I hid, like a dying wolf falls away from the pack.

All my books were out of print. All my words were dust.

I went to work as a maid because I had no other way of paying my bills. Too proud to ask for help, but the newspapers found out: "Once-famous writer works as a maid."

Research. That's what I told them, and flashed them all a big smile.

I had to quit before week's end.

My mother used to say an enemy had sprinkled travel dust around the doorstep the day I was born. I traveled so far to come back home. Never stopped loving the world, just stopped expecting it to love me back.

Some things I do regret.

One is that I didn't have the strength to gather up all my papers before coming here. Now eight hundred pages of Herod will be thrown out with the trash and burned to a crisp before they rent out the house. That's my own fault. I thought I had more time to put my things in order. But everyone knows how I feel about bothering people with my problems, especially when they have enough of their own. I thought I could take care of it by myself.

Then there's Lucille. I saw myself in her. Did she ever read what I wrote about her? That I loved her and would have trusted her with the US Treasury? She would have liked that. I always wondered what happened. I'm sorry I never wrote her. Never guessed one book could lead to so much trouble. And back then I wasn't ready to die.

Behind a curtain, they wheel out a bed of salty, twisted sheets. I don't want them to draw mine. They wouldn't understand my tears. If only they could see what I see.

With each breath I float higher, in a flutter of light.

I exhale. My dream is finally true.

I inhale. There's less of me, and more of you.

With one last breath, I soar.

Papa Legba, you divide heaven and earth. Open the gate for me. I'm
coming home to that little girl by the side of the road.

JANUARY 1, 1937

Soup for All

The first two days of the year
we celebrate
our independence.

We were the first
to unchain ourselves
and create our own country;
on the first day
of 1804,
we declared Saint-Domingue
free and renamed it
to honor the first people,
who called it Ayiti,
the land of mountains.

The first day of the new year,
I cook soupe joumou
the way Cousin Phebus
taught me.

I wake up early
to peel and cut
the calabaza
into even squares,
then cook the pumpkin
in water

with beef neck bones
marinated in
Scotch bonnet peppers,
pikliz, and lime.

The sharp smell of the soup
winds through the house
as I add cabbage and leeks
and roll flour in my palms
to shape the cloud dumplings.

I'm glad Cousin Phebus
brought me her recipe.

I tell Mamzelle it's a
Haitian tradition
to eat this soup
on January 1,
and to offer it
to anyone
who comes to the door.

Soup is even
served on the streets
of cities for anyone
who asks.

Though I haven't finished
cooking today's meal,
I have to prepare
the real feast.

Independence Day

Mamzelle says
she loved La Gonâve
but right away saw
that Faustin Wirkus story
of being crowned
the White King
was a fraud.
Still, it sold
a lot books
for him
and William Seabrook.

She adds that she, too,
wants to sell many copies
of the book
she is writing about Jamaica
and Haiti,
but she will do that
with the truth
instead of more lies.

Of course
I don't tell her
I dreamed of her dying
alone.
What good
would that do?
But it has shaken me,
and made me look at her
with a tenderness
I didn't really feel before.

At midnight,
we watch
the fireworks
light up the capital.

Mamzelle and I make a toast
and sprinkle champagne
on each other
and on the earth,
for the ancestors.

JANUARY 2, 1937

Ancestry Day

A juicy African guinea fowl
is our feast
on January 2,
the day that honors
all our ancestors
who fought
for our independence,
the day the president
addresses the nation
at the big parade.

Mamzelle says
she doesn't want
to hear any more
of President Vincent's lies,
so she's staying home.

"Rumor has it
he wears makeup to look as white

as he can. His grandmother
must be rolling in her grave!"
She loses herself
in her laughter.

So she *has* been talking
to people who trust her.

I chop up beets and carrots
to make a salad
in the form of a cross,
my own silent prayer
to find Fifina this year.

JANUARY 7, 1937

Enough for a Month

The past few days,
I've been preparing
for our journey north,
to La Citadelle,
cleaning the house,
buying provisions,
and packing.

"Pack enough
for a month,"
said Mamzelle.

The Feast of the Epiphany
came and went,
with an epiphany
of my own.

I have an idea.

I'll get Mamzelle
to go to Cazales
to see if my dream of Felicia
will help me find Fifina.

At least Celestina
did give me that clue
that Madame Ovide
could be from Cazales.

What if Madame Ovide
was the well-dressed woman
the doctor saw
helping Fifina?

What if
she took Fifina to Cazales
to keep her safe
from the section chief?

Oh, Celestina. We could have been friends
if you hadn't betrayed me.

Mamzelle agrees
to this new stop on her trip
right away.
"I like places like that,
off the beaten track.

"We leave in two days."
She rubs her hands in excitement.

"I have some big plans
but can't tell you more."

So do I.

Fifina. Oreste.
Will I see you again?

Thank goodness
at least Papa and Tante Lila
are safe.

Both hope and fear
take a seat in my gut.

JANUARY 8, 1937

Between

Mamzelle gets a letter
that makes her smoke
all her cigarettes
in just one morning.

"Ah, Henry Moe!"
Mamzelle sighs,
pushing away the envelope
on the table.

"Who is he?"

"The man who gave me
the money to do
my work here. He's from
the Guggenheim Foundation,
a place where
white people with money
give away some of it
to people like me.

"He's waiting for
a report on my research.
How can I explain that
writing
a book about voodoo
is like trying to squeeze
a whole universe
into a postcard!

"And he doesn't know
my novel came first."

Her novel,
the one she was celebrating.

"Am I in it?"
I ask, in a way that's
half joking.

"Yes, you are.
Because your culture,
and those who serve
the spirits,
the colors, trees,
symbols, and numbers,
are all there
for those who know
how to look.

"But I don't think
most readers will see
that what I've learned
in my fieldwork
is the heart
of my novel.

"My heroine,
like Erzulie Frida,
the lwa who lives her life
for love.
She also
has three husbands.

"When she finds
the love of her life,
he's younger, like mine.
Together they work
the land,
in a place called the muck.
They fight, too,
like I did with my love.

"Eventually she must kill him,
because he catches rabies
when he's attacked by a dog
during a hurricane."

"The one you left behind
in New York?"
I ask, thinking
what would I give
to see Oreste again.

"I had to leave him,
like I told you.
He thought he could dictate
how I should live.
We were either fighting
or making love.
I chose to be free."

"That sounds
like a passionate story,"
I say.

That also sounds
like Mamzelle does not care
what people think or say
on the teledjol.

She goes into her bedroom
for more cigarettes.

"Lucille," she says, lighting
a new one, "you'll never really be free
without money of your own.
I've been able to write
this novel,
and am writing my book
about Haiti and Jamaica
and starting my autobiography,
because for the first time in my life,
I have money
and freedom."

So it's not true
that all Ameriken
are rich.

"A few years ago,
a rich white woman
I called Godmother
sent me money
every month,
to gather my people's folktales
for her.

"But the price was my freedom.
I had to send her
a list of everything I bought,
even Kotex.

"It's not like that
with the Guggenheim grant
I have here
and Mr. Moe."

I must make enough money
from my carvings
to open my school
to have freedom
and help others get it.

"I've already told him that
I—*we*—will go down in history,
for taking the first photo
of a real zombie."

Mamzelle sent her photos
of Felicia
to a magazine
called *Life*,

though zonbis
live in the space
between death and life.

Clinging to the Cliff

The next morning,
we leave for Cazales,
which I can't even find
on Mamzelle's
large tourist map.

We head north
on la route nationale,
which connects the capital
to Cap-Haïtien,
more than a hundred miles away,
says our map.

But in the wrong weather
or with bad luck on the road,
you can never be sure
how long it will take
to reach where you're headed.

The car slowly climbs
past the weathered cacti
up the steep mountains
to Arcahaie.

On our left
is the sea,
in which I want to swim
one day
when it's warmer.

It's too chilly now;
I wrap my shawl
tighter
around my shoulders.

It's my first time
using a map.
I stare at it
to try and find my bearings,
the way I did
with the numbers in math.

Of course,
I don't say this to Mamzelle.

Instead, I memorize the directions
we get at the petrol station
at Arcahaie.

We've driven
less than twenty miles,
says Mamzelle.

Yet it already feels
like we're in
another world.

"Mamzelle, this is where
Catherine Flon,
Dessalines's goddaughter,
sewed the first Haitian flag
in 1803, the one we celebrate
every May 18 on Flag Day."

Now I'm the one
teaching Mamzelle,
and I like that.

She slides her sunglasses
down her nose,

and gives me a
wide-eyed look.

"So you're willing
to be my guide?"

"Why not? I'm learning
a lot from this."

I hold up my copy
of *La Voix des Femmes*.

"Uh-huh. Professor Lucille,
you can translate some of that
for me while I drive.
Unless you'd rather
hear more of my stories."

We both laugh
because we know
her stories
never end.

Unmapped

We leave the car
with the petrol station's owner,
and hire a local guide
to show us the way.

We travel
on the back of a burro,
Mamzelle in khaki trousers,
her old wide-brim hat
shielding her eyes from the sun.

I'm wearing pants
Mamzelle gave me,
trimmed to my size.

I like them a lot better
than the shadow-girl uniform
I had to wear at Madame Ovide's

or the dresses
Tante Lila sewed for me,

except for my Sunday dress,
which she made from the cobalt cotton
of my mother's dress.

Mamzelle said
we'd be more comfortable
in pants, and she's right.

I hold fast to her waist
as the burro moves slowly   across a wide, shallow river
littered with rocks,
not a bridge in sight.

On the other side—
Cazales,
a village of stone
clinging to a cliff.

Even the scrub bushes
look thirsty.

The burro sways
under his load.
Some loose stones
bounce down the mountain.

"Welcome to the glamour
of fieldwork!"
Mamzelle says,
chuckling.

Burros remind me of home.
To me, this is already special,
like the way Oreste said he felt:
we are explorers
in our own homeland.

Dried-mud houses,
banana-leaf-thatched roofs.
Triangle houses,
carved balconies,
not like any
I've ever seen.

Off the burro
we shake out our legs.

Villagers stare
from a respectful distance.

Mamzelle opens her canvas bag
with her red notebook,
her field recorder,
and her camera.
I think of Oreste again—
that dinner party
was just a few months ago
but feels like another world.

Untying the bandanna
on my head,

wiping the sweat
from my face
and neck,
I prepare for my mission.

Find my way
back to Fifina.

Silence
and stares.

A village
on the moon.

Their Reward

Here
the villagers look strange,
lighter than Madame Ovide,
but their faces are freckled.

Women with thick brown braids
pinned on top of their heads.

The village elder steps up,
leaning on his walking stick.

His accent in Kreyol
is too hard for Mamzelle,
so I take my place in the center.

"This Ameriken
is writing a book
about our country
and needs your help.

"Can she ask you
some questions?"

I wait to ask
about photos
and recordings.

Mamzelle digs in her bag
for a dollar.

The elder
waves it away.

"We will help her
if she helps us."

Mamzelle agrees,
not waiting to hear
what kind of help they need.

Grateful

"My great-grandfather's name
was Stanislaw Zalewski,
but everyone here
just calls me Granpè."

Mamzelle writes quickly
in her notebook.
"How old are you?"

Granpè strokes
his cloud-white beard.

"We measure time here
by the people in power.

"I was born
under the rule of Faustin,
emperor of Haiti."

Not the faux Faustin,
that White King of La Gonâve!

If Fifina were here
she'd do the math quickly.
His face is lightly lined,
his eyes like Madame's.

Sometimes old people
grow back into children.

Granpè leads us
past a cemetery,
strange names on headstones:
Belnoski, Kanski, and Lovinski.
On one of them,
we see a large
six-pointed star
with pebbles lined up
on the headstone.

"Our people came
from the land
of Polska."

"La Pologne?"
I ask, remembering
Sister Gilberte's
map of Europe
in her books.

Granpè nods,
leans on his walking stick.
"Napoleon sent
my grandfather's unit
to accompany
his brother-in-law
General Leclerc
so they could recapture
Saint-Domingue for the French."

He talks slowly
so Mamzelle can write
it all down.

"Aah, but the people here
refused to be recaptured.
They wanted to keep the freedom
they'd fought so hard for.

"My grandfather understood
this, and laid down his weapons
to join the people.

"Napoleon's rising debt
led to his sale of
the Louisiana Territory.

"Ameriken like you
should be
grateful to Haitians for this,"
Granpè says to Mamzelle.

She looks up from her notebook,
her pen in midair.

Forgotten

"Thank you, Granpè.
You sure know your history!"
says Mamzelle.

Mamzelle is a campfire
that draws people
to her.

Granpè smiles wide
beneath his beard.

"I am the guardian of the stories.
I remember it all,
and I teach the young
to remember, too,
so that when I die,
the stories live on."

"What happened
to the other Polish soldiers?"
Mamzelle asks.

"Most died of yellow fever.
A few hundred survived,
and the great Dessalines
decided not to have them killed
since they had refused
to shoot unarmed men.

"Instead, he gave them all
small plots of land
to farm in this region,
and together they built
this village.

"My grandfather
always said the Poles
knew what it was like
to fight for their nation."

Polska had been
invaded over and over again,
Granpè explains,
but the Poles had never given up
their struggle for independence.

The Polish soldiers could see
that the Haitians were like them.

Slaves wanted freedom
as much as they did

and they were willing
to die for it.

Like the Poles,
our people put their faith
in the promise
of the French Revolution:
liberté, égalité, fraternité.

Were they wrong to have faith?
What is it like to live
forgotten
by the rest of the world?

Their Church

Granpè stops when
we reach the church,
leans against it.

"We have no records,
no proof this land is ours.

"We need help
to feed ourselves,
to keep our village
from dying.

"The land isn't irrigated
and the crops can't grow.

"We cut down our trees
and sell them at market,
but when the lavalas come,
there are no trees
to prevent the mud
from washing away our houses.

"No one in La Pologne
knows we exist.
The Haitian government
doesn't care.

"All we have left
is our church,
our music and dances,
and a handful of stories."

Mamzelle asks Granpè
about a proverb neither
of us could figure out.

"'Mwen chage kou la pologne.'
What exactly does that mean?"

"It means,
'I'm in excellent shape,
ready to take on the world.'

"Our soldiers
who joined the Haitian army
were well trained.
We fought with our guns
and our brains.

"And here is our treasure,
our church," he says,
sweeping his arm
across the threshold.

A leaking roof,
rotting wood floors,
cracked and dusty
stained-glass windows

and yet
the villagers
are proud
their church
is still standing.

"We need help
to make our repairs,"
says Granpè to Mamzelle.

"Most of our young people
leave
to work in the city.

It's hard to farm here.
Would you be
so kind
as to petition
President Vincent
on our behalf?"

Mamzelle carries herself
in a way that suggests
she would have
the president's ear.

From the Fire

Granpè leads us
to the front of the church.

"The original
Black Madonna
            is in Polska
            in a place called
            Czestochowa."

He pulls back
a faded velvet curtain.

Long oval face,
long, thin nose,
almond eyes.

The brown child she holds
wears a heavy jeweled crown like hers
with two angels supporting it,
but his crown has a cross
at its center.

"The one in Polksa
was painted
by Luke the Evangelist
on a tabletop
built by Jesus,"
says Granpè.

I can see Mamzelle
has her doubts,
but she says nothing.

The scars
on the Madonna's cheek
are a darker brown,
like her eyes.

Her skin is the color
of cherrywood,
a little bit darker
than my hand.

I've never seen
a Black Madonna before.

"Why is this
Madonna black?"
Mamzelle asks Granpè.

"They say a fire
started in the church.
Everything burned
except our Madonna.
It was a miracle!"
He looks up to the sky
and makes the sign of the cross.

On the Porch

We leave
the Black Madonna
behind her velvet curtain.

Across from the church
an old woman
watches from a
long wooden porch.

"That reminds me
of back home,
where people told stories,"
says Mamzelle.

I hardly hear her.
The old woman's eyes
draw me to the porch.

In my knife pouch
is a copy
of my drawing of Fifina,
carefully folded.

I pull it out,
hand it
to the old woman.

"Bonjou, ma kòmè,"
I address her as Godmother,
as Papa taught me,
as a form of respect
and to remind us
that we are all connected
in a web of caring.

"Have you seen
my friend?"

The woman's glassy eyes
stare straight ahead,
and I wonder
if she is blind.

"Yes. She was here."

*If she's blind,
how can she know that?*

"Ma kòmè,
did you *see* her?
How do you know
she was here?"

"It's true
my eyes can't see.
But I know she was here.

"She never told me her name.
She said an evil man
was hunting her
and she needed to hide.

"She was here,
then she left."

My knees start to buckle
again,
as they did
at the hospital.

"Was she alone?"

"No. Belle Madame
brought her.
She told us
to keep all of this secret."

"Who is Belle Madame?
Where did my friend go?"

A shrug.
"Sorry. I can't remember
anything else.
At my age . . ."

I can't tell if she's lying
to keep her promise.
Her face closes
like a window shutter.

Is it possible
that Madame Ovide
brought Fifina out here
after she lost her baby,
one of those times I thought
she was with Jeanne Perez?

Shouldn't I
have noticed something?
But I was too happy
she was gone,
so I could spend
more time with her son.

The woman
hands me back
my drawing.

I want
to scream
cry
pray
for help.
Ask the Black Madonna
for another miracle.

Whatever power
I felt I had,
the faith that my dreams
tell the truth
is draining away,
drop by drop.

Fifina, why won't you
show me
where you are?

Erzulie Dantor

After saying goodbye
to Granpè and the villagers,
Mamzelle tells me
she's happy
I suggested
this wonderful detour.

"You do realize
that Black Madonna
is also a shrine
to Erzulie Dantor?"

Mamzelle is excited,
recharged.

"She's the lwa of
vengeance, who
inspired the slaves
to revolt in 1791.

"From our ancestors' gods
and the Church of Rome,
something new
was created."

Our *ancestors?*
So now
she's one of us?

"Someone once told me
you had to choose
between the Church
and our gods,"
I say.

"That someone
was wrong.

"Don't let anyone
shrink your horizon.
Make it
as wide as you can."

The Black Madonna

I am she who cannot be shamed or shackled. Believe me, they tried.
Rejoice and be glad that they failed.

They tried to banish me into darkness.
In darkness I dwelled and bided my time.
I watched and waited.

Time is a spiral I watched uncoil from beginning to end
and back to beginning.
Stone earth tree sky water sun stars,
and back again.

I held myself back until time was right.
Blessed is the fruit of my womb, my roots, my limbs.

Night water black. Long before the flames in that church.
Black as the earth's center.

My womb is a waterfall cave.
My fingers are trees that touch the sky.

I know you saw me in Mapou. When I spoke, you listened.
That's why I'm here.

I'll tell you a secret no one else knows.
I grew tired of waiting in shadow.

I am the spark that lit the fire.
I am the fire that lights the way home.

Ma Kòmè

"Why was that old woman
 on the porch
 sitting all by herself?
Why didn't she join everyone
 else when they went in the church?"

Mamzelle shrugs.

"Maybe she did something,
 they considered taboo,
 like help other women
 throw away their babies,
 or maybe she sold
 her very young daughter
 for a very high bride price.
Or maybe she just didn't
 play by the rules.

"There are many things
 that can label you
 a sinner
 or a witch."

Her father was a preacher.
So does Mamzelle
believe in sin?

Am I a sinner
for the ones I love?

That night my dreams
are as blank
as a parched cliff
in the dry season.

Ghosts

Mamzelle is as eager
as I am
to see
the ruins of Sans-Souci Palace
when I read its history aloud.

She grips the steering wheel
with one hand,
her cigarette
in the other.

In this perfect weather,
we can make it
to Milot in one day.

"The palace took twenty years
to build, but
King Henry the First,
as he called himself,
to honor the British
and their abolitionists,
didn't live to see it finished.
The king shot himself
with a silver bullet
rather than suffering a more painful death
by his enemies' hands.

"His wife was Queen Marie-Louise,
and their two daughters,
Anne-Athénaïre and Françoise-Améthisse,
were princesses,
not much older than me,"
I read from the magazine.

Mamzelle grins.

"The Black Royals,"
she says. "I wonder
what it was like in that court."

If I were a princess,
Madame would be only too happy
for me to marry her son.

"Judging from what I've read,
I'd guess it was opulent.
Our last queen and princesses
were allowed to leave
and live in England,
where people say
they met that other queen.

"It's a good thing
King Henry didn't live
to see the earthquake
destroy what was left
of his dream."

To see past the surface
is a gift
and a curse.

What They Did Not Teach Us

"Of course
there were kings back in Africa,
before we were stolen away
to be slaves.
There are even slaves in the Bible.

White people didn't invent slavery,
but they sure made it worse,"
says Mamzelle.

"They didn't teach
us any of this
in the Mission School,"
I say.
"Did they teach you
that at your school?"

"Yes, but Howard University
was a special school.
The professors were like us
and wanted us
to know our history."

"We need that here,
so everyone can learn
that when we declared ourselves free,
we were forced
to pay back the slave owners
for the slaves they had lost,
and we're still paying!"

Mamzelle shakes her head.
"The world isn't fair."

That,
I know.

"One day I'll start
my own school,
with my friend Fifina.
We'll teach all of this
and more."

Mamzelle's eyebrows rise,
but her smile is serious.

"We can make magic
when we make up our minds."

Names That Are Waiting

Toussaint, Henri Christophe,
Dessalines, Pétion.

Names baptized in blood.

There were many women
in our revolution:
Sanité Bélair,
Catherine Flon,
Marie Sainte Dédée Bazile,
Marie-Jeanne Lamartinière,
Cécile Fatiman,

but their names
might be forgotten

as Cazales has been

if we don't fight
to keep them alive.

The queen
and her princesses,
Erzulie Dantor,

names tucked away tight
in the bindings
of books

waiting for freedom
and light.

The names from our past
aren't written in books.

They will fly like blackbirds
from the pages of books
when I open my school.

A New Kingdom

"They need to pave
the road to Milot,"
says Mamzelle.
Her car shakes
in complaint
as it climbs.

When we do reach
Sans-Souci,
Mamzelle
goes off with a guide.

I want to walk
the haunted hallways alone.

In the ruins
of the palace,
I close my eyes.
Couples dance
in a circle,
their fingertips touching.

Beneath
waterfall chandeliers,
they curtsy and bow
to the king and his queen.

Newly made royals,
barons
in bicorn hats,
purple plumes

at attention.

For their loyalty,
land and islands,
favors from a king
who was once a slave.

King Henry
imagined
a new kingdom
for the Africans
who'd been
stolen
from their own.
He wrote to the
king of England
and others
to make sure
the slave trade would end.

When we visit the Citadel,
it's even more impressive
than I imagined.

"No wonder it's called
one of the world's wonders,"
says Mamzelle.

She has me
take a photo
of her
posing on a cannon.

We stand
shoulder to shoulder
staring over the parapet
out over the ocean.

To build
this mighty fortress
and carry heavy stones
up these steep hills,
were people forced,
the way sòlda Ameriken yo
used corvée workers,
treating us like slaves,
during the Occupation?

Or did we work together
of free will, in harmony,
like a konbit?

All of this, to keep out
invaders, and slavery.

But isn't debt
a way for slavery
to slide by
all the cannons?

All the awe the king
hoped to inspire
with La Citadelle
would just lead
to bitterness, suspicion,
and the desire to destroy.

No wonder they want
to keep making us pay
instead of building schools.

Every morning
before Mamzelle
wakes up,
I carve
from Papa's ebony.

Now I see
that history
is another way
of finding
shapes in wood.

FEBRUARY 5, 1937

City of Dreams

That afternoon,
after leaving the Citadel,
Mamzelle drives us
speeding on the road
to Cap-Haïtien,
Le Cap,

a city of dreams
built on canals

the Venice
of the Caribbean.

We arrive at sunset.

The houses here
are painted in
cheerful pastel
yellow, blue,
lavender, and pink,
decorated with
delicate balconies
of wrought iron.

Mamzelle's in a rush.

"I have an important meeting
in half an hour
at the Hôtel Impérial."

She shifts the
Ford's grumpy gears.

"Come on!
Don't break down
on me now!"

Mamzelle turns left
at the last minute,
almost climbing the curb,
at the hotel's front door.
The bellhop rushes out
to carry our bags.

While I unpack,
Mamzelle unfolds her map
and checks against something
in her red notebook.

"I hope this informant
can help me
find where the meeting
will be tonight.
Alan gave me his name."

"What meeting?"

"The less you know,
the better,
but I'd still like you to come
in case
the French or Kreyol
is tricky."

I agree.

Ambition

I've never seen
Mamzelle this excited.

"I've been asking myself
about what Germany
would do here
if there's a war,"
she says
as I help her
fasten the buttons
on the red silk dress

she wore for Mesye Alan
and smooth down her hair
with her flat iron and pomade.

My hair is easier
to care for
now that I keep it short.

I'll wear my
Sunday dress,
the blue one
Tante Lila
sewed for me,
using the cloth
of my mother's dress.

Since leaving Madame Ovide's
I always wear
my mother's sandals.

"I ask questions
for a living,
the perfect cover
for a spy,"
says Mamzelle.
She laughs,
but her voice
sounds nervous.

"I could even
help President Roosevelt.
I could be his special adviser,
like Mary McLeod Bethune,"
says Mamzelle.

"Who is she?"

"Her parents were enslaved.
But now she's the president
of a college in Florida,
the place I told you about,
where I grew up.

"Only in America
could that ever happen."

If Mamzelle
takes me to America,
could I also run my own school,
where Oreste would teach history,
and we could be married?

First things first.
I must find Fifina.

Informant

In the hotel lobby,
I wait with Mamzelle.
In the shade
of potted palms,
colorful paintings
hang on the wall.

I lean in close
to one painting
to see every detail.

A market woman
walks alone,
her basket
on her head,

climbing a mountain
where sky
and earth meet,
blue green red
paint, alive
in the frame.

At the bar, Mamzelle
meets a Haitian man in a suit,
wearing glasses,
hunched over his drink.

Mamzelle slides next to him
and asks the barman
for a rum punch.
I ask for a glass of grenadine juice,
to remind me of
my special day with Oreste.

Mamzelle orders two lambi dishes
with rice, banan peze and pikliz.
I can't wait to devour
this special meal.

The informant glances around,
takes off his glasses
and wipes them
with a white handkerchief,
then puts them back on.

He points out
a spot on her map;
Mamzelle marks it with an X.

I pretend
I'm not listening
as I sip my juice.

"President Trujillo's army is
massing at the border,"
the Haitian man whispers.

"Does President Vincent know?"
asks Mamzelle.

The man stares hard
and leans in.
"Do you know
Jacques Roumain?"
he asks.
"He was trying to help
the dockworkers, the planters
at the American sugar company,
all the workers, getting them organized
into unions to fight for their rights.
First time they arrested him,
only a hunger strike
led to his release,
and he fled to New York. But he returned.
Vincent's secret police followed him
everywhere,
and now he's back in jail,
accused of wanting
to overthrow the government.

"His health is getting worse.
You can imagine.
We're doing all we can
with comrades all over the world

to get him released.
He would already be dead,
if his family wasn't so powerful.
Remember his grandfather
was once president,
before the Occupation.

"If they could do that to our Jacques,
think of what they can do
to people like me."

Jacques Roumain.

I remember that name,
from Oreste's letter.

The server's
black-and-white uniform
reminds me of the one
I wore for the dinner party,
except he wears white gloves.
He sets down our plates
with a flourish.

I start cutting my lambi
without waiting for Mamzelle.
It's perfectly tender,
with a sauce of
tomato, onions, and scotch bonnet peppers
as good as Cousin Phebus's.

The informant stands up
to leave and shakes
Mamzelle's hand.

"No need to tell you
this shouldn't be shared,"
he says before leaving.

Mamzelle stares into the mirror
behind the bar, then
turns around quickly.

"Did you see him?"
she asks, her face frozen.

"Who?"

"The one from the secret police
who
threatened us.

"He's here."

"The man with the
pince-nez? Here?
Are you sure?"

I look around the room
and don't see him anywhere.

"I think I just saw him
in the mirror.

"Let's get out of here
before it's too late."

"What about our dinner?"

"Leave it.
We don't have time."

The Border

We rush up to our room.
"Pack everything back up.
We're not staying here.

"We're leaving
for the border
near the Dajabón River,"
Mamzelle says,
out of breath.

It's dark when we get there.

I can't tell how many
people are gathered,
in this hidden forest
clearing, lit by small torches.

We sit on a carpet
of soft green pine needles.

A man appears,
in a farmer's straw hat
and stands under
a giant cedar tree.

I can't see his face,
but he's wearing
a clean white shirt
and smooth trousers,
not like any farmer
I know.

The people grow quiet
as soon as he speaks.

"Mes konpès!
Mes kòmès!

"We know that our land
was a Garden of Eden

"but what we see now
is a paradise fallen."

His voice quiets
and stills us,
like a griot
around a fire.

"We've had enough
of Trujillo's brutality,
how his police and soldiers
arrest us,
beat us,
jail us.

"They say we don't have ID cards
or residence permits,
and they make us pay twice
for documents
we never needed
at the border
until Trujillo took power.
They won't even let us
take care of our own farmland
and our animals
across the border.

"They say we're selling contraband
or stealing,
but what they're doing

is trying to label us
and make people believe
we are all criminals.

"We're tired
of Vincent's duplicity,
letting Trujillo visit our country
as if he's a friend
when in fact,
Trujillo calls us filth
and says his hygiene laws
are the reason for his crackdown
at the border.

"We're tired of having our hopes
dashed on the rocks
of poverty

"of corrupt politicians
in league
with greedy corporations
like the Haitian American
Sugar Company.

"It's time
to stop complaining.

"It's time
to start fighting
corruption and greed,
wherever we find them.

"When we work together,
just like the konbit
when we're clearing a field

or building a house,
no one can stop us.

"The big fish is used
to eating small fish,
but when small fish
swim together
they can chase
the big fish away.

"The future is ours!"

His fist
punches the sky.

The people rise up
everyone clapping.

I jump to my feet
blind with excitement.

I know that voice!

Underground

I push through the crowd
to that voice in the center.

Oreste blinks in surprise,
then reaches out
and pulls me to him.

"Ti Zwazo? What
are you doing here?"

We move away
from the others.

"Shush. Please wait.
My comrades told me
where we can hide.
There will be police
looking for me."

We stoop down
to brush away branches,
and we enter a cave.

My hurt and anger
are tangled.

"Why didn't you tell me
you were back?"

"How could I?
My own mother
doesn't even know
I'm here.

"I'm working with farmers
to fight for their land.

"Our president says
people like me
are Communists
so they can blame us
for everything,
when it's their
greed and corruption
that is hurting our country.

"If they find me,
they'll throw me in jail,
and torture me

to make sure
they scare others."

That smell of fear
when I went to the police station
and felt the ghosts of the prisoners
sends a wave of nausea
through my body.

"Just tell me what happened."

I lace my fingers in his.

"My comrade told me
that back in January,
yon fanm Ameriken
wrote a letter
the government censor read.

"They went ahead
and let us meet
because they want
to capture our leader
and arrest him,
like they did
Jacques Roumain."

His words skip the river
of fire inside.

Yon fanm Ameriken.

*Could she have posted
this letter herself?*

"That's terrible!"

There's no way
I can tell him
I suspect Mamzelle.

"Even so, couldn't you
have sent me word?"

Oreste lowers his head.

For a second,
I'm afraid
of what he will say.

The Cave of the Lost

When he finally answers
he looks straight in my eyes.

"I didn't want us
to fall in love.

"I knew that one day
my life
would be
this."

A bit late for that.

"Your letter
from New York?
You already knew
back then?"

That single word *servants*
still stings.

"I thought
you'd understand
what I meant
when I wrote about
Central Park and
the birds."

"I did understand,
but I just wasn't sure."

"In New York,
I met people who showed me
how to make
real change happen."

Our foreheads are touching.
We stand holding hands,
our breath warming each other.

"Your friend? Did you find her?"

"No, but I'll never give up."

He lights his lantern.

"These are Taino
carvings,"
he says.

"My grandmother was
part Taino,
and they never let us
go into the cave."

"Well, you're here now,"
he whispers, and I
turn to kiss him.

We devour
each other's lips
and let our hands
roam
all over our bodies

until he rests his head
on my shoulder.

"I missed you,"
he whispers.
"You don't know
how much."

"As much
as I missed you,"
I say,
stroking his hair.

Our voices
soft echoes.

"I love you,
Ti Zwazo,
and always will."

Time
doesn't feel real
in this cave.
If only
we could stay
here
forever.

On the walls
around us

are carvings and paintings.
Heart-shaped faces
with big eyes,
swirling like water
holding us
afloat.

The world
of our ancestors,
kept hidden from us
right under our feet.

Escape

"We don't have much time.
Can you find a way
to get me
to the harbor?

"I know a comrade
who will sneak us
on his fishing boat
and take us to Cuba,"
he says.

"I'll ask the woman
I work for
to give you a ride."

"Too risky. I could be
recognized. They've sent out
my photo."

"I have an idea.
Take off your clothes,"

I say as Oreste
kisses my neck.

His eyes still look like
seeing me is a miracle.

"Ti Zwazo, I'd love to,
if only we had more time."

"Just take off your clothes,
and I'll take off mine.
Then we'll switch."

We stand up
and face each other.
I take off his shirt,
kissing his smooth
naked shoulders and chest,
then step out my dress.
His eyes stroke me
from top to bottom,
warming me
from deep inside.

I hand my dress to him,
he puts it on,
then I wrap my red mouchwa madras
around his head.
A few curls peek through.

I put on his shirt and trousers.
They fit my gazelle body well.

We hug tight,
then hold hands
at the mouth of the cave.

"Will you come with me?"

My heart nearly stops

as I hear the words

I've always wanted to hear.

Night Ride

I ask Mamzelle
to drive us to the harbor
as fast as she can.

She looks at us both,
but for once,
she doesn't ask any questions.

Mamzelle tells him
to sit in the front.
His smooth hairless face
is framed by my madras.

I sit in the back
in his straw hat.

His soft white shirt
and warm jeans,
caressing my skin,

still hold his scent
of pine and eucalyptus.

I wish
none of this had happened,
that we could be back

in our courtyard and garden,
our paradise lost.

Mamzelle slows the car.
Up ahead we see lanterns
sweep the darkness,
and hear
men's voices barking.

"Police. Must be a checkpoint."
Mamzelle's voice is steady.

I put my hand on Oreste's shoulder,
his hand touches mine.

We know these may be
our last seconds together.

Checkpoint

The car rolls to a stop.

The police.

Each second a heartbeat.

> If Oreste runs, they'll shoot him.
>
> If he doesn't, they may drag him away,
> to who knows where.

Knots coil tight
in my neck and chest.

Mamzelle rolls down
the window,

"Bonsoir. What's going on here?
Sorry, but those are the only
French words I know."

I'm grateful to see
how Mamzelle lies as well
as an actress.

"Do you speak
English?"
she asks.
She tilts
a cigarette from her pack.

Oreste turns his face
away from the flashlight
that rifles the car.

"Merci, Madame,"
says the police officer
as he puts away his flashlight,
takes the cigarette
from Mamzelle's box,
and stares at it hard.

"*Pall Mall!* Américaine?"

Mamzelle smiles
and nods. Lights up her own.

A second policeman
comes up to her window.

"You're an American?"
the second man asks
in English.

He's clearly the boss;
his rifle is shining.

"Yes, I'm an American,
all the way from New York.
Please keep the pack."

The boss thanks her,
puts the pack in his pocket.

"What are you doing here?"

"Enjoying the sights."
Her voice doesn't show
any footprint of fear.

"La Citadelle. What a
magnificent fortress!"

The boss finally
breaks open a smile.

"Yes, it is. The pride
of our people."

"With good reason,"
says Mamzelle.
"So can you tell me
what's going on here?"

"We're looking
for a fugitive from the law,
a real troublemaker."

"What has he done?"

"Many bad things.
He spreads lies
about our president."

The boss shines
his flashlight on me.

I hold my head higher
to bury my fear.

"Well, he's not here,
as you can see,"
says Mamzelle.
"These are the servants
I hired for my stay.
It's late. Can we go now?"

"Of course, Madame.
Enjoy the rest of your stay
in our fine country."

"Thank you, Officer.

"I sure hope you find him.

"The world doesn't need
any more lies about Haiti!"

She waves goodbye
and rolls up the window.

"Close shave,"
Mamzelle says quietly.
"Too close for comfort."

It's the first time I'm grateful
for my gazelle body.

Open the Gate

No one talks
until Mamzelle
at last breaks the silence.

"Little men with big guns
don't scare me.
When I was driving around
the South collecting stories
in a car I called Sassy Susie,
I used to carry a gun.
Never had
to use it, but traveling around
alone as I did, things could
have gone very wrong.

"As they almost did
back there."

Oreste reaches back.
His fingers touch mine.
We lace them together.

"A close shave, all right.
Things can go wrong
just like that." Mamzelle snaps her fingers,
then glances at me
in the rearview mirror.

"Thank God
I was initiated
and know a special prayer
to Papa Legba, the god
of the crossroads. I asked him
to throw open the gate.

"We call on him
at the start of every ceremony, like this:

"Papa Legba, ouvè baryè pou lwa yo!
Ayibobo!"

Mamzelle's voice sounds teasing—
and relieved. "Papa Legba,
ouvè baryè pou nou antre.

"I asked Papa Legba to
help us all find a way."

My breath
is no longer shallow.

For once I am happy
Mamzelle
serves the spirits.

A Harbor in Moonlight

The full moon
shines, ripples
on the skin of the sea.

At the checkpoint,
I thought
I'd lost him again.

Now is my chance
for love
and to fight
what's unfair.

That rickety fishing boat
holds
our whole future.

Mamzelle stays in the car
on the lookout for us

in case they decide
to search for him here.

We're still dressed
in each other's clothes.
Oreste
lifts my blue dress to his knees
to step onto the boat.

"¡Hola, compañero!
There are two of us
coming. I'll explain later."

The Sea and the Flame Tree

Part of me wants
to hop on the boat,
and follow you
wherever you're going

a warm soft vision
of us floating
on a raft of flowers.

My other dreams
are knives to the heart.

Finding Fifina
going back to school

carving my sculptures
in a house by the sea.

My day-night dreams.

If I follow you
to your dream,
would I lose my own?
Would your love
die as fast
as the flame tree blossoms?

When tangled dreams
meet at the crossroads,
which do you follow?

Love pulls at me,
urgent and hungry.

I dip my bare feet
in the seawater.

"We don't have much time,"
says the fisherman.

You're already
untying the rope
from the dock.

You reach for my hand
to pull me onto the boat.

I hold your hand tight,
but my feet stay
where they are,
feeling the mapou trees

and the caves
calling me back.

Clouds shift
across the field
of your face.

> *If I don't go with you now*
> *I may never see you again.*

"I'm sorry. I thought
I could leave—"
The words are stones
in my throat.

"I didn't *want*
this to happen,"
you whisper.

Every inch of my body
longs to sail our horizon.

The dream of my school
feels small in comparison.

But is it, really?

Our ancestors
fed us, body and soul.

And Fifina.

I can't leave
until I've done everything
to find her
and free her.

"Ti Zwazo, I understand.
This life isn't for everyone."

We hold each other
 again, not wanting
 to let go.

"I'm not afraid.
 But I have to stay,
 to find Fifina,
 to start our school,
 or die trying."

We kiss like fugitives parting,
 each second more precious.

"Compañero. It's time."
The fisherman doesn't shout.
There's respect in his voice.

I let go, step back on the shore.

"I'll always love you,"
 you say. When you step on the boat
 it rocks under your weight.

"I won't stay away long.
 When I return, I'll come
 teach in your school!"

You pull out my carving
 from your knapsack,
 kiss it, hold it up high.

I knew you still had it.
And it did keep you safe.

In my dream
of you
in the water,
I was a tree.

I dreamed the truth.

Again.

A tree split by lightning
may never mend.

My tears
blur the boat
as you grow smaller
into the night.

Sick

I ride back with Mamzelle
to a pension
where she's booked a room.
She says she feels tired
and needs to
go to bed.

Being away
from Oreste now
is worse than it was before,
because it was my choice.

I sniff his hat
for the scent of his hair.
I will wear his hat
whenever I can.

The cliff in my heart
is now a ravine
filled with love's ashes.

The next day,
Mamzelle stays in bed,
feeling sick.

"What did you eat
on your own that
I didn't eat?"
she asks me.

"Nothing. We had the same
meal at the hotel.
But didn't you have a drink
at the bar?"

Mamzelle's forehead
is sticky and hot.

She vomits into
the bucket I hold.

"Belly. Cramps. Poison."

Words she spits out
between shallow breaths.

"They know   the photo   Felicia.

      "They   know   what I've seen.

           "They followed us   here."

Pince-Nez.
The drinks at the bar
of the Hôtel Impérial.

I didn't have a rum punch.

Could they really
have poisoned Mamzelle?

The Letter She Wrote

At sunset,
Mamzelle closes her eyes.

"Of course they've
been reading my mail."

Sometimes she took
her own letters to the post office
and picked them up there.

"I wrote a letter
to my friend in New York,
a famous writer.
I was so excited
something important might happen,
I told her to drop everything
and join me here."

My eyelids twitch.

At first I think
she can't be the one.

But now
it all makes sense.

It was *her* letter
that tipped off the police.

If they knew about the meeting,
the secret police could have found out
that Oreste would be leading it.

Mamzelle is the reason
Oreste had to leave.

Mamzelle is the reason
I had to choose.

My Pencil a Knife

All that time
I was so busy
   teaching her Kreyol
   searching for Fifina
   wishing for Oreste

I forgot

Madame Ovide's warning.

Don't trust Mamzelle.

And now Mamzelle
has proven her right.

It's Mamzelle's fault
Oreste had to go.

I let that sink in.

My temples are pounding.

I rip out a piece
of her notebook paper,
my pencil a knife
of vengeance and fire.

Note for Mamzelle

You said you loved truth.
You told me, have faith.
But your heart is full of poverty.
You throw down your thunderbolt wherever you want.
Your camera is a cannon.
Your notebook is filled with battle plans.
Even with our machetes and ancestors' prayers,
we had no chance.
Yet you asked for my help,
and I gave what I could.

Rotten teeth feel strong
on soft bananas.

I wanted to help you
find what you were looking for.
You could not see it.
You thought it was in the eyes of a zonbi.
You said you were here to make things better.
You said you could save lives.
You said so many things
I wanted to believe.

You said you loved truth.
You told me, have faith.
I should have known you would lie.
It's time that you go.

Wildfire Rage

I keep the note
with my knife
in the leather sheath
Papa made.

Mamzelle is no better.
She sleeps on and off.
When she's awake
her talking is wild.

There's no telephone in
this little pension.

I wake up the owner downstairs.
She has no idea
where to find a phone
at this hour. Offers to have
her husband go for a doctor.

But Mamzelle doesn't want that.

"Don't you understand?
They all want to kill me!"

Mamzelle's nails
dig hard into my arms.

"Don't you remember,
the man who threatened

Joseph? When he was
in the kitchen,
what did he say?"

"Nothing.
He just wanted some rum . . ."

"You're lying!"
shouts Mamzelle.

> *Is lying the same*
> *as not telling*
> *everything you know?*

"Let go!
You don't know
what you're saying."
I twist away from her hands.

"The Secte Rouge,
a secret society.
The police
and the government man.
The checkpoint.
You're in on it, too?"
whispers Mamzelle, eyes wide
and bloodshot.

I stumble backward
away from the bed.

Fear feeds the sickness.

That must be the reason.

After I saved her life
by keeping her away
from the drums in the night.

But with the sickness,
Mamzelle won't believe
a word that I say.

She's in
her own world

where I don't exist.

Where can I get help
up here in the north?
I don't know a soul
in Le Cap.

Madame Ovide,
Cousin Phebus
are both too far away.

My volcano inside
erupts,
with the lava of rage.

Put the note
by her bedside.

And leave her.

Vigil

Most of me
wants to leave
wildfire rage
burning my body
but a still, quiet voice
I can hear only
with the ear
of my heart

> tells me
> to
> stay.

No Doctors

Mamzelle is
too weak
to sit up in bed.

Since she accused me
of lying,
there hasn't been one word
between us.

I bring
her chamber pot,
mop the sweat
from her face and neck.

Bring her
cassava and milk.

Nothing works.

"I *have* to get
you a doctor. Can you
give me some money?"

But Mamzelle insists,
"No doctors. Can't trust anyone.
They'll finish me off."

Night Forest

If she won't let me
find a doctor

I'll have to
be one myself.

I rifle through
Fifina's recipes
for an answer.

Nothing.

Recipe book
under my head,
I fall asleep

and wake

from a dream
of the forest

where Oreste
gave his speech.

Papa's words sound
as if he is here.

Find the shapes
in the wood.

Running back
to the forest
for a sign

any sign.

Sweating
and panting,
looking around
for a clue.

Only this tree
in front of me,
a growing mapou.

I wrap my arms
around it

put my ear
to its bark

and listen.

The Mother Tree

Mapou told us to care for you

as we care for each other.

Take out your knife,

take a piece of my skin

from my roots, take the mushrooms.

You'll have what you need.

Together

The mushrooms
I gather
from the forest
aren't ones I know,
but the smell is familiar.

I'll make a tizan,
and try it out on myself
first.

I run back
to Mamzelle.

"Don't let them
cover the clock,"
she whispers.

"When Mama died,
they covered the clock."

If I take what I have
on hand,
I can make
something new.

"Don't take the pillow,"
she says before crying.

I take
a handful of dried hurts-your-hands
a cleaned forest mushroom
and a sliver of mapou bark

boil water to steep them

and pray.

Carving Dreams

Just because you've lost me
doesn't mean I'm gone.

My roots are like fingers gripping the earth.
My roots are rivers that flow underground.

You were in night water. I watched from the shore.

They want to stamp my passport and send me right over.

When you see dry bones by the side of the road,
don't forget they used to be flesh and blood.

Don't know how I survived.
Bondye must have spared me for a reason.

I am she who cannot be shamed or shackled.
Believe me, they tried.
Rejoice and be glad that they failed.

Just because you've lost me
doesn't mean I'm gone.

Quiet

Mamzelle sips
the tea that I made.

I break up
a bar of soap
in a pan

pour in
her rum

set it on fire.

I burn up my note
in the flames.

> When it's cooled down
> I spread the mix
> on her stomach
> even on the ravine of her scar.

> I rub in a circle
> like the rings of a tree.

> Mamzelle flinches.

> I soak two compresses
> in the burnt
> rum and melted soap,

> place one under
> each armpit.

> A still, quiet voice.

> A faraway dream,
> lit from within.

Wait

I follow Mamzelle's
ragged snores

until she makes a sound
like a red-bottomed bird.

"Lucille."

A spoonful of tea
to her lips.

She sips it
and closes
her eyes.

Next morning
Mamzelle is awake.

"What happened?
I thought I was dying."

She stretches her arms;
dry compresses drop.

"What are these?"

"The medicine
I made for you."

Mamzelle sees me again

her eyes brimming with tears.

"Another close shave."

She's no longer sweating.
Her breathing is steady.

"I'm going back to America
as soon as I can. I'll see
a doctor I trust there."

I can't help remembering
her accusation.

"You said I was lying
and trying to kill you."

"I was delirious."

She pulls me to her
for a hug.

"I'm sorry, Lucille.
There are so many
secrets I know

"that people
don't want me to tell

"in my book.

"Whatever happens
I'll make sure that
nothing I write
will ever hurt you."

Mamzelle asks for her bag.

She pulls out her billfold,
and hands me
a twenty-dollar bill.
The only other one
I've ever seen
was at the market

when Madan Sara
dealt with the Ameriken.

In my mind,
I write the numbers in the air.
One hundred gourdes!
I've never seen
that much money
in my life.

"I want you to have this.
This is how much
I'd pay you
for the time I'll be gone.
Take it now."

A plan shapes in my mind.

"Mèsi anpil.
I will find Fifina.
I will go back to school
and one day start my own.
I'll even learn
enough English
to read your book."

"I don't doubt it
for a second,"
says Mamzelle.
"You remind me
of me
when I was your age."

News

And so it is
the next morning,
Mamzelle drives me to Le Cap,
where I will board the bus
to Port-au-Prince.

Only this time,
I'm not crying.

"You can stay in the house
I rented from Madame Ovide
until the end of the month.
I paid up before leaving.

"Now please just get going,
because I can't stand goodbyes."

Even then I know in my gut,
I'll never meet
another woman like her.

I cover that hurt
with a shawl.

The trip back to the city
goes by in a blur.

Mostly I sleep.

I stop at the market
to see Madan Sara.

"Lucille! It's been so long.
I was wondering if
a lougarou ate you!

"Mèsi Bondye you're here
and healthy.

"Here's the money from all
the polish and sculptures.

"I saved it for you.
Celestina doesn't come by
anymore."

She hands me
a thick envelope.

"Don't open this here.
You never know who
might be watching
and will follow
a young girl home
to rob her.

"Your cousin told me
the section chief
from your village
had a car accident
on the way to Cazales.

"That's a dangerous road."

*Can it really be true
that nightmare is over?*

"I hope you're still carving
because Madame Williams,
the artist, left her calling card.

"She said she met you
at Madame Ovide's.

She buys so many
of your carvings,
and wants you
to come to her atelier
for free classes."

My heart skips ahead
as I try to absorb
all her words.

Isn't all of this
a bit more than luck?

"Your cousin will be
so happy to see you.
She cooks at the new home
and girls school
Jeanne Perez and her friends
from La Ligue just opened.
Here's the address.

"Good luck!"
says Madan Sara,
before returning
to one of the blans
lined up at her stall.

Home

It's nearly dusk
when I reach the address
Madan Sara gave me.

There's a mapou
at the crossroad.

Her song blooms inside me
wherever I go.

I follow the path
that leads to the house
and knock at the door.

Cousin Phebus answers.

"Are my eyes playing tricks,
or is it
my ti cousine?"

She pulls me in
for a hug.

The sun in her heart
shines bright
just like mine.

"What are you doing here?"
she asks.

"I want to meet the director
to pay for school fees.
I've saved enough money,
and I could work, too."

"So you *are* smart!
But this school is free
for girls like us.
That's why I'm here.

"And listen to this: Your father
and Tante Lila
are moving to the city,

Madame Ovide got him a job
working on the cathedral.

"Don't ask me how,
but she knows
you helped
save her son's life."

"Now, please tell me.
How did you
end up here?"
I ask.

"I will. But first,
there's someone
I want you to see."

She walks me to the kitchen,
to the scent of dous lèt.

At the stove
a girl turns
to face us.

"Ti Sè."

Your voice is the same,
wild honey and butter.

But your eyes tell a story
my body hears first.

Stolen, you escaped.
Wounded, you rose

and opened the gate
at the crossroad.

We hold each other,
rocking to stillness.

I knew that I'd find you.
We're home before dark.

What We Don't Know:
The Story Behind the Story

This novel is set in Haiti from 1934 to 1937, right at the end of the nineteen-year US occupation. It's inspired by real events — and by a mystery surrounding them.

First, the real: Zora Neale Hurston went to Haiti on an anthropology fellowship in 1936. While she was there, she wrote her masterpiece, *Their Eyes Were Watching God*. And in her nonfiction book on Haiti and Jamaica, *Tell My Horse*, Hurston praised a Haitian woman named Lucille, who worked as her domestic.

Now, the mystery: Nothing else is known about the real Lucille. And Hurston's fieldwork notebooks have vanished.

Enter the magic of the historical verse novel. It has the power of intimacy and emotional resonance to paint history in primary colors.

In centering Lucille's story, I was largely inspired by three sources:

-→ the stories my mother told me about her grandmother, a bold market woman who lived through the occupation and narrowly escaped serious trouble

-→ the mystery of what happened to Hurston in Haiti, including her fear that her research on zombies was leading to trouble

-→ the work I witnessed by Chavannes Jean-Baptiste, the first Haitian winner of the Goldman Environmental Prize, whose anti-corruption activism did get him in trouble. Good trouble, as John Lewis would say.

Historical fiction is storytelling anchored in the past. Whenever possible, I tried to stay faithful to the historical timeline of major events, such as the withdrawal of US occupying forces in 1934, the 1936 summer Olympic Games in Berlin, and Hurston's first period of fieldwork in Haiti, from fall 1936 to spring 1937. I am greatly indebted to historians Yveline Alexis and Brandon Byrd for their assistance in getting the history right. Any remaining errors or omissions are mine.

Based on my research, I invented the characters and the stories of Lucille and her family, the section chief and his mother, the Ovide family, Celestina, Fifina, Cousin Phebus, and Pince-Nez, among others.

I took the liberty of placing the Black choreographer, dancer, and anthropologist Katherine Dunham in Haiti in 1936 for the fictional Madame Ovide's dinner party, although Dunham was not in Haiti at that time. In her letters, Hurston wrote often of Katherine Dunham in terms of a rivalry, pushed to compete against each other by their respective mentors, the anthropologists Franz Boas and Melville Herskovits. Unlike Hurston, Dunham made Haiti her home for decades, and she was eventually honored by the Haitian president for her contributions to Haitian culture. I gave her a cameo as a foil and to introduce some of the other real figures who represented Haiti's "talented tenth," to use the intellectual activist W. E. B. Du Bois's term. Du Bois himself was of Haitian descent.

The Haitian notables gathered at Madame Ovide's are among the many who worked for a democratic civil society and promoted the serious study of Haitian culture. These included the anthropologist Jean Price-Mars, sculptor

Hilda Williams, editor Jeanne Perez, along with others in the women's rights movement, and the prominent Sylvain family, particularly Suzanne Comhaire-Sylvain, the first female Haitian anthropologist.

I cast author and activist Jacques Roumain as an older role model for Oreste Ovide. His biography, *A Knot in the Thread: The Life and Work of Jacques Roumain*, by Carolyn Fowler, also helped me imagine how the Ovides might have lived.

When the Mapou Sings is about a lesser-known period in history that is relevant to our uncertain times. History is a song that enriches us all as more voices are included. Today there are young people like Lucille, Oreste, Fifina, and Phebus who are fighting every day to create a thriving Haiti and who are beacons of hope.

Bibliography

Notes on Selected Sources

For me, writing historical fiction took patient detective work and obsessive curiosity. As a historian by training, I'm particularly drawn to primary sources. Here are some of the key resources that helped me imagine a world I could never visit. Full citations follow as needed. For more information, please visit www .nadinepinede.com.

The statement from the US secretary of state on page 7 is from Address of the President at Cape Haïtien, Haiti, July 5, 1934, and "Final Ceremonies in Haiti," *Marine Corps Gazette*, November 19, 1934, a copy of which was shared with me courtesy of Professor Yveline Alexis, Oberlin University, and the original of which is held at the United States Marine Corps History Division Archives in Quantico, Virginia.

A helpful "Tourist Map of Haiti," drawn by M. P. Davis, was used by the American "song hunter" Alan Lomax during his visit to Haiti in 1936–1937. It's included in the ten-CD boxed set *Alan Lomax in Haiti, 1936–37: Recordings for the Library of Congress*. The set also includes Lomax's *Haitian Diary*, in which he recorded his meetings with Zora Neale Hurston. Some of Lomax's film footage from Haiti is available on YouTube.

The songs I included are folk songs I heard during my time at the thirtieth anniversary of the Papay Peasants Movement. Modern acoustic guitar versions of "Latibonit" and "Mesi Bondye" by Haitian American Leyla McCalla are available on YouTube. The lyrics of "Choucoune," known in Haitian Creole as "Ti Zwazo" and in English as "Yellow Bird," were written in 1883 by Haitian poet Oswald Durand.

A book of postcards of Haiti from 1895 through the 1930s, edited by Peter C. Jeannopolus, stimulated my imagination.

The photo Hurston took of Felicia Felix-Mentor, which she identified as the first photo of a zombie, appeared in a 1937 *Life* magazine article, "Black Haiti: Where Old Africa and the New World Meet."

Regarding Hurston's fascination with zombies, an article in *Medium* by Charles King, drawn from his book *Gods of the Upper Air*, on groundbreaking anthropologists, including Hurston, was an eye-opener for me. Science would suggest that Hurston was on the right track in her research, but only decades later; see Gino Del Guercio's article cited in the bibliography.

Very few letters written by Hurston from Haiti still exist. I relied on Carla

Kaplan's *Zora Neale Hurston: A Life in Letters* and letters written by Hurston in Haiti to Henry Moe, at the Guggenheim Foundation.

Hurston's niece Lucy Anne Hurston put together a sparkling collection called *Speak, So You Can Speak Again: The Life of Zora Neale Hurston*, which includes facsimiles of Hurston's handwritten notes, as well as early poems, painted postcards, and a CD of songs and interviews.

My mother's great-uncle Arsène V. Pierre-Noel wrote the first book on the healing properties of Haitian botanicals, called *Les plantes et les legumes d'Haïti qui guerissent.*

Some first-person accounts from Americans were useful, such as US Marine Corps Captain John Huston Craige's "Haitian Vignettes" and US Marine Corps Major G. H. Osterhout Jr.'s "A Little-Known Marvel of the Western Hemisphere: Christophe's Citadel, a Monument to the Tyranny and Genius of Haiti's King of Slaves," both of which appeared in *National Geographic.*

I expanded my knowledge of the rich tradition of Haitian proverbs with Edner A. Jeanty's *Paròl granmoun: Haitian Popular Wisdom: 999 Haitian Proverbs in Creole and English.*

Sources

Address of the President at Cape Haïtien, Haiti, July 5, 1934. Collection FDR-PPF, President's Personal File, 1933–1945, Franklin D. Roosevelt, Papers as President, Franklin D. Roosevelt Presidential Library and Museum, Hyde Park, New York.

Bell, Beverly. *Walking on Fire: Haitian Women's Stories of Survival and Resistance.* Ithaca, NY: Cornell University Press, 2001.

"Black Haiti: Where Old Africa and the New World Meet." *Life,* December 13, 1937, 26–31.

Bontemps, Arna, and Langston Hughes. *Popo and Fifina: Children of Haiti.* New York: Oxford University Press, 1993. First published 1932 by Macmillan (New York).

Boyd, Valerie. *Wrapped in Rainbows: The Life of Zora Neale Hurston.* New York: Scribner, 2003.

Craige, John Huston. "Haitian Vignettes." *National Geographic,* October 1934, 435–485.

Davis, M. P. "Tourist Map of Haiti," drawn for *Haiti, a Brief Historical Review and Guide Book* (1933).

Alan Lomax Collection, Manuscripts, Haiti, 1936–1937, Library of Congress. https://www.loc.gov/resource /afc2004004.ms120274/.

Del Guercio, Gino. "The Secrets of Haiti's Living Dead," *Harvard Magazine,* January– February 1986. https://www .harvardmagazine.com/2017/10 /are-zombies-real.

Dubois, Laurent. "Who Will Speak for Haiti's Trees?" *New York Times,* October 17, 2016. https://www .nytimes.com/2016/10/18 /opinion/who-will-speak-for -haitis-trees.html.

"Final Ceremonies in Haiti." *Marine Corps Gazette,* November 19, 1934.

Fowler, Carolyn. *A Knot in the Thread: The Life and Work of Jacques Roumain.* Washington, DC: Howard University Press, 1980.

Hurston, Lucy Anne. *Speak, So You Can Speak Again: The Life of*

Zora Neale Hurston. New York: Doubleday, 2004.

Hurston, Zora Neale. *Dust Tracks on a Road: A Memoir*. New York: Harper Perennial, 2006. First published 1942 by Lippincott (Philadelphia).

———. *Folklore, Memoirs, and Other Writings*. Edited by Cheryl Wall. New York: Library of America, 1995.

———. *I Love Myself When I Am Laughing . . . And Then Again When I Am Looking Mean and Impressive*. Edited by Alice Walker. New York: Feminist Press at CUNY, 1979.

———. Letters to Henry Moe. October 14, 1936; January 6, 1937; April 5, 1937; May 23, 1937; September 24, 1938; March 20, 1937. John Simon Guggenheim Memorial Foundation, New York.

———. *Tell My Horse: Voodoo and Life in Haiti and Jamaica*. New York: Harper Perennial, 2009. First published 1938 by Lippincott (Philadelphia).

———. *Their Eyes Were Watching God*. New York: Harper Perennial, 2006. First published 1937 by Lippincott (Philadelphia).

———. *You Don't Know Us Negroes and Other Essays*. Edited by Henry Louis Gates Jr. and Genevieve West. New York: Amistad, 2022.

———. *Zora Neale Hurston: A Life in Letters*. Edited by Carla Kaplan. New York: Anchor, 2003.

Jeannopoulos, Peter C. *Port-au-Prince en Images/Images of Port-au-Prince*. New York: Next Step Technologies, 2000.

Jeanty, Edner A. *Paròl granmoun: Haitian Popular Wisdom: 999 Haitian Proverbs in Creole and English*. Port-au-Prince, Haiti: Presse Évangélique, 1996.

Jennings, La Vinia Delois. *Zora Neale Hurston, Haiti, and Their Eyes Were Watching God*. Evanston, IL: Northwestern University Press, 2013.

King, Charles. *Gods of the Upper Air: How a Circle of Renegade Anthropologists Reinvented Race, Sex, and Gender in the Twentieth Century*. New York: Anchor, 2019.

———. "When Zora Studied Zombies in Haiti." *Medium*, July 23, 2019. https://zora.medium.com/when-zora-met-zombie-dbcf0fb45d11.

Lomax, Alan. *Alan Lomax in Haiti, 1936–37: Recordings for the Library of Congress*. San Francisco: Harte, 2009.

Lyons, Mary E. *Sorrow's Kitchen: The Life and Folklore of Zora Neale Hurston*. New York: Athenaeum Books for Young Readers, 1993.

Martin, Alain, dir. *The Forgotten Occupation: Jim Crow Goes to Haiti*. 2 Hander and Pameti Films, 2023. http://theforgottenoccupation.com.

Moylan, Virginia Lynn. *Zora Neale Hurston's Final Decade*. Gainesville, FL: University Press of Florida, 2011.

N'Zengou-Tayo, Marie-Jose. "Fanm Se Poto Mitan: Haitian Woman, the Pillar of Society." *Feminist Review*, no. 59 (Summer 1998), 118–142.

Osterhout Jr., G. H. "A Little-Known Marvel of the Western Hemisphere: Christophe's Citadel, a Monument to the Tyranny and Genius of Haiti's King of Slaves." *National Geographic*, December 1920, 469–482.

Paris, Robel. *Haitian Recipes*. Port-au-Prince: Henri Deschamps, 1955.

Pierre-Noël, Arsène V. *Les plantes et les legumes d'Haïti qui guerissent: mille et une recettes pratiques*. Port-au-Prince, Haiti: L'État, 1960.

Plant, Deborah G. *Zora Neale Hurston: A Biography of the Spirit (Women Writers of Color)*. Westport, CT: Praeger, 2007.

Simon, Scott. "Haitian Soup Joumou Awarded Protected Cultural Heritage Status by UNESCO." NPR, *Weekend Edition*, December 18, 2021. www.npr.org/2021/12/18/1065477169/haitian-soup-joumou-awarded-protected-cultural-heritage-status-by-unesco.

Tarter, Andrew. "Trees in Vodou: An Arbori-cultural Exploration." *Journal for the Study of Religion, Nature and Culture* 9, no. 2 (April 2015), 87–112.

Timyan, Joel. *Bwo Yo: Important Trees of Haiti*. South-East Consortium for International Development, 1996. https://pdf.usaid.gov/pdf_docs/PNACA072.pdf.

Twa, Lindsay J. *Visualizing Haiti in U.S. Culture, 1910–1950*. Burlington, VT: Ashgate, 2014.

Williams, Hilda. *Hilda Williams: un hommage*. Exhibition catalog. Port-au-Prince, Haiti: Musée d'Art Haïtien, Ateliers R. Jérôme, and Centre d'Art, 1995.

"Zora Neale Hurston: Claiming a Space." PBS, *American Experience*, 2023. https://www.pbs.org/wgbh/americanexperience/films/zora-neale-hurston-claiming-space/.

"Zora Neale Hurston: Jump at the Sun." PBS, *American Masters*, 2009. https://www.pbs.org/wnet/americanmasters/masters/zora-neale-hurston/.

With All My Gratitude

First, a big thank-you to the intrepid teachers and librarians who invite us to explore the past and imagine our possible futures. I am profoundly grateful to the many people who helped bring this book into being. Rubin Pfeffer faced unexpected challenges on this book's journey with unstinting grace and wit. He has been a genuine inspiration to me. Amy Thrall Flynn has been a generous and patient guide, as well as a friend. My deepest gratitude to my dedicated editor, Carter Hasegawa, whose breadth and depth of cultural knowledge and sensitivity made revision feel like flow. All my thanks to the fabulous team at Candlewick Press and those working with them, including Hannah, Stephanie, Dana, Sasha, Nicole, Elise, Nathan, and everyone else I wish I had the space to include your name. You gave my book the best home, and your warm welcome during my visit was unforgettable. My heartfelt gratitude for the timely and invaluable assistance of Alison Hall, Gail Bloom, and Lainey Cameron, whose advice to use my joy filter touched me at just the right moment.

Archivists and biographers were vital to this journey. I'm grateful to those at the Beinecke Rare Book & Manuscript Library at Yale University, where I saw Hurston's handwritten draft of *Their Eyes Were Watching God*—and the many crossed-out passages in *Tell My Horse*! Seeing those pages sparked my imagination. Were the redactions made because Zora was afraid of the repercussions her research might have, or did she fear for those left behind, like Lucille? Thank you to the Guggenheim Foundation archives for mailing copies of Zora's correspondence. At the Fashion Institute of Technology, director Valerie Steele kindly showed and let me touch the kind of clothing my characters would be wearing. Thank you to Zora's biographer, the late Valerie Boyd. She graciously responded to my emails, as did Lucy Anne Hurston, Zora's niece.

Thank you, Lucille, for inviting me to unearth your life, and Zora, for trying to support yourself as an author, which remains a challenge today. I still recall the thrill of discovering Jamaica Kincaid's "Girl" in the New Yorker and thinking, How did she do that? When I was in college, Alice Walker inscribed my copy of In Search of Our Mother's Gardens with one word underlined three times in purple ink: Be! Toni Morrison told me to "stay the course." The best advice is often the hardest to follow.

Thank you to my early readers and supporters, including Cristina Garcia, Breena Clarke, and A.J. Verdelle. Elizabeth George, the mystery writer best known for her Inspector Lynley series, awarded me a grant from her foundation and later funded a fellowship that allowed me to attend a low-residency master of fine arts program. Thank you to all the students and faculty of the MFA program at the Northwest Institute of Literary Arts, which is unfortunately now shuttered. It was a joy to learn from David Wagoner, Kathleen Alcalá, Carolyn Wright, and Bruce Holland Rogers. The extraordinary Edwidge Danticat, a MacArthur Fellow, served as my thesis adviser and later selected an excerpt from my MFA thesis for her anthology Haiti Noir. Her encouragement and generosity over the years, and her brilliant work, including her historical novel The Farming of Bones, have all helped me more than I can say. The same is true of Tananarive Due, award-winning author, professor, screenwriter, and executive producer of the documentary film Horror Noire. I thank whoever assigned us as roommates for our New York Times summer internship!

I am deeply grateful to invaluable organizations helping writers in this challenging publishing landscape, such as the Authors Guild. The Society of Children's Book Writers and Illustrators helped me cross the bridge with its regional chapter and webinars and by awarding me a scholarship to its unforgettably inspiring annual conference. A big thank-you to George Brown and the Highlights Foundation family. Thanks to a scholarship, my manuscript found its shape at a Whole Novel Workshop led by Ashley Hope Pérez, author of the historical young adult novel Out of Darkness, one of the most challenged and banned books in the United States. It was also at Highlights that the ebullient novelist and workshop leader Nicole Valentine read my very rough draft revisions and offered lucid suggestions, as well as remarkable kindness.

Thank you to Kip Wilson, Jeannine Atkins, Cordelia Jensen, and Lyn Miller-Lachmann, who led me to discover the powerful beauty of the verse novel. Emma Dryden showed me the potential of returning to a manuscript I'd considered abandoning. Lesléa Newman's loyalty, encouragement, friendship, and editorial acumen helped me reach the finish line, in the shadow of grief. Marilyn Nelson encouraged me to not play it safe.

My mentorship with the exceptionally big-hearted Stacey Lee—thanks to We Need Diverse Books, which helped me write this new chapter of my life with both this mentorship and a grant for a summer working at Serendipity Literary Agency with Regina Brooks—gave me a compass to navigate challenges I didn't know were coming. And Stacey never once complained about our nine-hour time difference, which made our FaceTime calls feel like pajama parties!

Artist communities are sanctuaries that balance the gathering of kindred spirits with the need for solitary musing. I'm deeply grateful for the grants, fellowships, residencies, and other supports I found for this novel as it was taking shape. Among the groups that provide support are Hedgebrook, Norcroft, Ragdale, Vermont Studio Arts Center, Atlantic Center for the Arts, the Squaw Valley workshops, Villa Dora Maar, the Château de Lavigny, Under the Volcano, Key West Literary Seminars, the Studios of Key West, and the Betsy Writer's Room. Thank you to my friends in Key West, especially Ros, Joyce, and Kris. Also in Key West, whenever I see the iconic Judy Blume, a longtime advocate for our freedom to read and a co-owner of Books & Books, I'm reminded of why we persist. Bethany Hegedus and the wonderful team at the Writing Barn and Courage to Create gave me a chance to share what I've learned on this journey.

This would not be historical fiction without the history. I had help from the best, including novelist Madison Smartt Bell. Professor Yveline Alexis graciously shared her impressive expertise and pointed me in new directions that helped me deepen the novel in unexpected ways. Thank you to Professor Patrick Bellegarde-Smith for sharing his photos of family and of Haiti's iconic gingerbread houses and to Professor Grace Sanders Johnson for introducing me to the roots of Haiti's feminist movement. Professor Brandon R. Byrd was also generous with his knowledge. A big thank-you to the Haitian Studies Association for too many reasons to list, among them a revelatory screening of *The Forgotten Occupation*, directed by Alain Martin.

My novel was also sparked by contemporary figures, such as the courageous activist Chavannes Jean Baptiste, whose advocacy for disempowered small farmers in Haiti earned him the Goldman Environmental Prize. It was a privilege to help support his activism with the Mouvement Paysan Papaye. My admiration continues to grow for the students, faculty, and staff of the Haitian Education Leadership Program, which fights Haiti's brain drain with the country's largest college scholarship program. Thank you to Conor, Sam, and Ian, who helped me establish a scholarship in memory of my mother, Claudette, for young Haitian women. Chapo to Berchie, our first scholar, whose own words about her own remarkable journey radiate fierce hope from which we can all learn. Thank you to Chancellor Emeritus Charlie Nelms and his wife, Jeanetta. Professor Nelms has been an avid supporter of the scholarship fund, a valued friend, mentor, and role model. It has been an honor to collaborate with him across the years.

I'm extremely thankful for my friends, extended family, and allies, including Abby, Suzanne, Erika, Dan, David, Carmen and her late husband Juan, Carole and John, Barry, Bob, Philippe, Dennis, Simon, Fifi, Mayra, Shelley, and all of my fabulous cousins, nieces, aunts, uncles, godparents, and other members of our marvelous family. Tonny's support has been especially generous. Although we live far from each other, we remain close in spirit. Thank you to my brother Didier "Ed" Pinede. He is a devoted dad, voracious reader, walking sports encyclopedia, and, like our mother, a riveting storyteller.

I doubt I would have completed this novel without the abiding love of my husband, Erick, who helped lift me at my lowest points. His love of music and his curiosity as a scientist are matched by his keen editorial eye and sense of humor. Our beloved Hoosier cats and our Flemish dog remind us every day to savor the joys of the present moment, even as I confront fibromyalgia and other invisible disabilities. My pain mentors, Frida Kahlo and Octavia Butler, continue to inspire me with their boldness and courage.

I'm grateful to my ancestors, including those who have joined them this past decade, especially my mother and my father, Edouard. He linked his passion for music with pioneering creativity as an engineer in the same way my mother joined her passion for stories and for poetry, which she could recite by heart, with her teaching, service, and faith. I am still dazzled by the beauty of the letter my father wrote in French asking for my mother's hand in marriage, and I return often to the wisdom of a letter he wrote me about perfectionism. My mother's enthralling stories of Haiti and her grandmother, Grandmè Mimise, inspired this novel.

My parents shared an exceptional zest for life, whose roots I witnessed in their homeland. Dèyè mòn, gen mòn, is one of Haiti's most well-known proverbs. Beyond mountains are mountains. Thank you to those who remain undaunted by the climb, guided by justice and compassion. Kenbe. Thank you to those who came before and who dreamt us into being. You made this possible, and I carry you with me. Mèsi anpil.